IRON CROW

THE CRAWLING GIRL
BOOK ONE

KIM PETERSEN

Whispering Ink Press

This is a Whispering Ink Press book brought to you by Whispering Ink Press.

Previously published as Rebellion, 2018.

eBook IBSN: 978-0-6489305-6-3

Paperback IBSN: 978-0-6489305-7-0

Edited by Jennifer Collins

Cover by Roy Migabon

❀ Created with Vellum

ALSO BY KIM PETERSEN

Blood Legends Post-Apocalyptic Vampire Thriller

Undead

Rebirth

Ascension

Ascended Angels Chronicles Paranormal Thriller Series

Millie's Angel

Angels & Vixens

Dark Soul

Untamed Destinies A Romance Anthology

Dark Shadows: Vampires and Ghosts of New Orleans Dark Fantasy Horror
Anthology

"It takes courage to grow up and become who you really are."
e. e. cummings

_T_ime stole our history, and the lake buried it. Even before I was old enough to understand the importance of the stretch of water along the shore, I yearned to be close to it.

I lived in a Hydran village—the old timers called it Gas Works. I'm not sure what that name means, but it didn't matter to us, those left behind. I knew most but not all the people in the village. At one time, there had been hundreds of families but now we numbered closer to 50.

I always loved the way the sun struck the massive steel and iron structures towering over our village. At some point, Lord Corvus had reserved this land for Hydrans, and we'd been there ever since.

When I was little, my grandfather would often say I was smart enough to run a Hydran village. Yet, his face would cloud with fear when he made such jokes. Then he'd tell me I was too stubborn for my own good, which wasn't a welcome trait to have for a politician. Being his little Rayna would always be enough.

Enough for what? I used to wonder, as I'd watch him ready for a day crawling the lake. I guess he meant it was enough that I become a Crawler like him.

The water had reclaimed most of the ruins by then, yet there had been a time when my grandfather witnessed something else. A time when the Seattle skyline soared high in the sky, and people had more than they needed and wasted things we Hydrans had to eventually fight for. Lives filled with an abundance of food, warmth, running water, and electricity. A time when the Crows hadn't perched atop Queen Anne Hill and no Lord Corvus ruthlessly ruled over our village with a sharp eye and a heartless regime.

My village struggled under Lord Corvus, yet I'd never known otherwise. I figure that's why I was always so drawn to the water.

Because, in the water, there was silence.

I'd felt most free while crawling, even if only for fleeting moments. I could become one with the water, and on some days, I knew that the lake's hidden secrets were the only thing to keep me going. Everyone in the village had a job or a responsibility starting as young as 12 years old. I'd been born a Crawler—a scavenger who dived for aluminum to trade to the Crows for food and resources.

I'll never forget that day as long as I live. It started like any other morning, but once I slipped beneath the surface, something felt different. During this particular dive, the secrets of Lake Union eluded me, and I tried my best to fend off my impatience.

I ignored the pressure in my head as my waterlogged fingers fiddled with the worn strap of my goggles, working fast to tighten the strap before the goggles filled with water. I released a timed breath into the snorkel as I swam further into the watery depths.

The early afternoon sun streaked through the murky water after me, catching particles along its cloudy columns. Normally, I would've taken a second to marvel at the way the sunbeams softened and spread through the water like a mantle of golden snow. But not on this day.

I'd been crawling for hours, with only a couple of nails and some foil to my name. Being a third generation Crawler, I'd rather not have revealed my catch to any other Hydran—not with *that* kind of haul under my belt. Especially not to Jaef and his goons. Not to mention the fact that I needed a decent load to trade because we were running out of food at home.

I hadn't crawled through this area for a few weeks, and I'd hoped the current had swept in some new loot, but I hadn't found any yet. After diving down a few feet further, I saw an opening that appeared to begin one of the ancient tunnels. Crawlers had discovered many of these underground passageways in my grandfather's time. They're dark and unmapped with uneven terrain, and only the best Crawlers have the guts to venture inside.

I stopped for a second and paddled in a suspended glide as I adjusted my Bright. I moved my head around to shine it in all directions. I'd had this Bright since I'd been a little girl, and it hadn't failed me yet. Some Crawlers had to constantly repair theirs—fiddling with the bulb or cracking open the case of their old light to check the wiring. I guess you could say that my crawling skill wasn't the only valuable thing I'd inherited from my family.

Something caught my attention in the depths a few feet into the tunnel. I wriggled closer to get a better look, curling my legs under me, feeling the surge of adrenaline rush through my veins as I saw a pile of cans through the murky water. Those old aluminum cans had become increasingly harder to find. A pile like this could fetch a week's worth of grain and, if I was lucky, maybe even enough to barter for a new strap for my goggles.

Using the arm with my Band on it, I reached toward the pile. A quick touch with the magnetized bracelet would tell me if the precious metal was aluminum versus iron or steel. The Crows only traded for aluminum, making anything ferrous worthless.

I turned my head from side to side, my eyes darting around to check for signs of other Crawlers. I knew I wasn't alone out here.

I had noticed Jaef and his crew preparing to dive earlier, and I'd deliberately avoided crawling near them.

With nobody around, I kicked my legs and sprang deeper into the lake, never losing sight of the gleaming, brilliant aluminum cans. As I approached the mouth of the tunnel, my skin erupted in goosebumps. The water became colder, but I didn't care. I focused on the heaped prize bundled against the rugged rocks near the tunnel, and knew it was mine.

The gritty bottom bloomed in front of me like a muddy cloud, and I lost sight of the loot. I frowned and then slowed down, blinking through the dreary puff that had just begun to dissipate. Narrowing my eyes and peering toward the aluminum, I felt a wave of relief washing over me when I caught sight of the cans twinkling through the dull light. I was about to dive down for the aluminum when I saw *them* in my peripheral vision.

Their bags trailed behind them along with a long line of bubbles as they swam ahead of me. That jerk, Jaef, and his crew had cut me off.

I wanted to scream, and I might have had I not had a mouthful of snorkel with only a whiff of breath left. Instead, I gritted my teeth and broke hard for the treasure on the tunnel bottom. My arms stretched as far as my reach would allow, and I kicked my feet with the fury of a wild tornado.

Another gritty cloud billowed up, and I lost sight of the cans again. I swam even harder, pushing through the murky water. The muscles in my limbs had become taut and strong, and I knew I could beat Jaef's group.

My head burst through the water cloud just in time to see Jaef shoving my find into his bag. I stopped, my heart sinking as my empty stomach growled. Jaef's blonde hair floated over his goggles as he stuffed the last of the cans into his bag. He tightened the drawstring and looked up at me, his teeth bared and crooked in a wide grin. He shot me a thumbs-up and then motioned to his crew, a flurry of bubbles floating all around us as they grinned at me.

I'd seen enough. I couldn't out-muscle all of them for the haul. If I didn't leave, I knew I might do something I'd regret. Like twisting my hunting knife into Jaef's kidneys. With that comforting thought, I turned from them and swam back to the surface and the spot on the shore where I'd jumped into the lake.

Soon it would be time to take my puny haul to the scrapyard and put it in front of the metal merchant. Maybe I'd come across a pile of scrap aluminum on the swim back and score enough for a little something for my grandfather.

By the time I dragged myself out of the lake, I'd almost forgotten about Jaef and his thievery.

Most of what rimmed the shore of Lake Union was left over from the old times. Some of the houseboats still floated on the surface, but most had sunk in the water and provided us with an almost endless supply of scrap metal. When the fog cleared, you could easily see across to the other side. People didn't live by the water anymore. At least not the normal ones. It smelled, and on long days crawling, I'd come out with a headache and blurry vision. I didn't want to know what was in the water because it didn't matter.

I crawled. That was my job.

I spotted Asher walking along the bank toward me, and I felt my face flush, my ears burning.

His full brows knotted together. "Hey, what's up?"

I used to be taller than my best friend, Asher, but he towered over me now. At twenty-four, Asher was three years older than me. Despite his age, people in the village called him an 'old soul,' and although I'm not sure exactly what they meant, he always seemed wise for his age. He stood at least six feet tall with strong, muscled arms, a lean build, and calloused fingers. And yet, his soft brown eyes and full lips made others feel at ease around him. Especially the girls. When Asher was a boy, he had what we call the wheezing. On hot days, he had a hard time breathing, and so he'd been assigned to work as a farmhand although I'm positive he would've been a great Crawler, had it not been for his condition. His dad passed away in a crawling accident, though, so I'm sure his mom was fine with him being assigned to the fields instead of the lakes.

Asher's smile faded as I strode closer, the filthy, cold, lake water dripping off me. My wet raven hair stuck against my forehead as my eyes narrowed. I tossed my diving gear aside and held up my dive bag, swinging it around for good measure.

"Jaef is what's up. Him and that idiot crew just stole a pile from right under my nose! They were following me, I just know it."

I threw the bag down near my diving gear as a snarled growl tore through my throat and rang in my ears. Falling to my knees beside it, I let my hair cover my face.

Asher's hand brushed my shoulder, and I looked up at him through tears I hoped were masked by the water.

He shook his head and smiled. "There'll always be more. Tomorrow the current will wash it in. My mother predicts a storm tonight."

It took everything I had to keep the tears from really flowing, but I hated weak people, and I didn't want to be one of *those* girls who needed a boy to comfort me. I swallowed the lump in my throat and studied my toes—white, wrinkled, and with the nail beds covered with grainy sand.

"Rayna?"

I looked up at Asher, seeing his lips curved into a smile as he reached for my face and traced the frown lines on my cheek with his finger.

"You know, if the wind changes, your face will stay that way, right?"

I laughed and shooed his hand away before standing up.

"You're full of shit." I reached down and gathered my diving gear.

"Maybe, but I got you to smile," he said, handing me my snorkel. "C'mon, you better get home and get cleaned up."

We walked to our village in silence, parting only when we reached the fork in the road.

Asher turned to me there. "Catch you later."

His smile had faded, and a heavy seriousness crossed his face.

"Yeah, okay. Thanks, Ash."

I watched him walk away before getting ready for the daily trip to the metal merchant. And like I did after every crawl, I turned and sneered in the direction of the Crows living their privileged lives in the Nest atop Queen Anne Hill.

---

a s I paused at the halfway point from the Lowlands to the yard, a light breeze blew thick and musty. I took a deep breath when I reached the shade of the maple trees that hung over the road. The hike up to the Kerry Park Scrapyard made my legs burn. I could never get used to the steep incline, not with pulling my haul behind me and the rope rubbing my hands raw.

I must have walked the road a thousand times, yet I never got used to climbing the hill. It didn't come with a payoff. I mean, it wasn't as if I was ascending to a promised land or the place my grandfather called heaven. No. This was an ascension to the gates that held the precious metals, and I had never seen beyond the wall. None of us had.

I just knew the metal merchant would screw me again, always haggling over the amount of aluminum or the exchange rate. Crawlers brought the metal merchant a haul, and he weighed it, then gave us what he considered a fair trade of food. My grandfather was a Crawler, as was his father before him. Nobody could really remember when the aluminum trade started, but that held true for many Hydran traditions.

The Crows had built the wall out of stones, chipped brick,

and mounded earth. It stretched high into the sky and completely enclosed the scrapyard as far as the eye could see. The scrapyard itself had been constructed with more thought than our village, and that should tell you all you need to know about the Crows who don't even live inside its walls. They built a small city called the Nest, another few hundred feet higher and sitting on top of Queen Anne Hill. And the leader of the Crows, Lord Corvus, doesn't even live in his own city. Along with his counsel and family, he rarely comes down from the top of the Space Needle which overlooks all of the ancient ruins and villages that have cropped up over the years.

My friends and I, we've all sat on the Troll, staring up at the Space Needle and making up stories about that crazy structure. Why is it there? Who built it? How did they build it? The old Hydrans claimed to know, but their stories seemed only slightly less ridiculous than ours.

My group hung out under the bridge in old Freemont where the Troll lives. He's not a real troll—just a sculpture that somehow survived war, famine, flooding, and time. Crow law prohibited us from handling weapons, but that didn't stop us from secretly practicing them in the dark recesses of Freemont. When you're 18 years old, you believe you are both invincible and beyond the rules.

I could hit a bullseye with my bow at 100 yards and even with his beady eyes, Jaef could do the same with a spear at 75 yards. We made sure to stash our weapons every night before returning to the village.

Sometimes we scavenged through the buildings still standing in Freemont, but they'd been picked clean over the decades. One time, Asher found an old picture of the Needle surrounded by buildings with electric lights and nestled in the comfortable palm of the Cascade Mountains. Honestly, it didn't look real.

"Watch out!"

Some Crawlers a few years younger than me had blown by on

their cart, riding it down the road with their food rations stuffed in the back. One of them almost knocked my legs out from under me, which would have spilled my cart.

"You watch out!"

My Crawler friends and I, we didn't do stuff like that anymore. It didn't seem as fun, the older you got. I waved my fist in the air, but they'd already coasted down the road and around the bend toward our village. I looked down at my measly haul. Two days? Three days? I'd be lucky if it fed my grandfather and me through the end of the week. The metal merchant was constantly tweaking the exchange rate as if there was some master mathematical equation he used to figure out how badly he was going to cheat us.

Looking up the hill, I didn't see any more Crawlers preparing to ride down, so I stopped and reached for my canteen.

Save some, I reminded myself. *Corvus has been rationing the well water.*

I stamped my foot down, watching the gravel and dust ripple around my boot. Then I looked at my rickety cart, and to the top of the gate, which I could see from my vantage point.

147 steps.

That's how many it would take for me to get to the front of the line and stand before the metal merchant.

I straightened up with a flick of my braided hair, ignoring the passing stares of other Crawlers passing me on their way to the scrapyard. Some carried their hauls in their arms, which made the ascent easier, but they'd come down with less food, as well.

Step 52.

That's where the line started. In my grandfather's day, only official Crawlers could trade their haul with the metal merchant. But now, anyone with a sack and a can claimed to be a Crawler, and the Crows didn't seem to care as long we kept bringing them their precious metal.

I stopped near a row of trees, panting and reaching for my

canteen but then leaving it on my belt. Even though I didn't have the haul I should have, thanks to Jaef and his squad of idiots, the cart weighed a ton, and no matter how many times I did the climb, it never seemed to get easier.

As I gazed around, my eyes fell on the armed guards near the gate with their rusty-looking leather jackets and steely faces. They yelled the same things at the same people—every single day. Corvis' guards had two jobs: protect the scrapyard and keep the Crawler riff-raff *far* away from the Nest. Hydrans had always been strictly forbidden to go anywhere near the Crow city. Other than the metal merchant, I can't ever remember even seeing a Crow.

Step 10.

At this point in the line, I could smell the body odor and moonshine breath of the metal merchant. He wore a leather vest over a ripped shirt and a bandana around his head that was so filthy you couldn't tell what color it had been. The man's exposed arms glistened with sweat over his tattoos—dark images of feathery black ravens, cryptic symbols, and half-naked women. He wore thin, black fingerless gloves, his burly fingers being tipped with blackened fingernails. When he tossed the scrap metal into waiting carts, his biceps flexed.

Step 1.

The guy in front of me turned and walked away with a pumpkin and two ears of corn. The metal merchant looked at me, his eyes creeping over my body like a deadly spider until they settled on my breasts. I looked down at my sweaty shirt clinging to my skin.

"C'mon, brown eyes. That's the best you could do?"

I couldn't tell if he was talking about the size of my breasts or the size of my haul. I guess it didn't matter.

"I've got almost as much in my cart as the man before me."

He leaned in closer with a hot, rancid, whisper that made me gag. "I got an officially approved exchange rate for Crawlers like you."

I stepped back, crossing my arms over my chest. "No thanks."

His lips curled as he pulled back.

"Whatever. Drop your haul. I don't have all day."

I dumped my cart on the scale and stepped back as the metal merchant slid the weight along the metal arm until he found the balancing point. He grunted while he emptied my loot into a cart waiting to go through the gate, and then he handed me a handful of beans, a half-rotted piece of broccoli, and three small potatoes before trying to usher me along with a wave.

I stood firm while the man behind me elbowed me in the back.

"What's this?"

"Your rations. Now, move along."

"But this is barely enough to feed a small child."

The big man chuckled. "Well, then maybe you should tell the others in your village to grow more food for us to ration. Now get!"

I'd opened my mouth to respond when an eruption of snickers and laughter came from further back in the line. I whirled around to see Jaef and his crew jeering at me through fits of titters.

One of his goons pointed in my direction. "Ha! Looks like Rayna got quite the return for her haul!"

Jaef's eyes caught mine, and he grinned. "Yeah, I reckon we all get what we deserve. Only the quickest get the pickings."

The group guffawed and taunted me as I stuffed my rations into my bag and tied it to my cart. As I grabbed the handle and turned it around, Jaef stepped in front of me.

"You got something you want to say to me? Or maybe to the metal merchant?"

I gritted my teeth and saw the metal merchant out of the corner of my eye—smiling and hoping to see a fight to break up the monotony of his job. I couldn't do that again—I couldn't afford the punishment that would leave my grandfather on his own. I swallowed a big, bitter, ball of pride and smiled at Jaef.

"We all know who's the best Crawler in the village."

I caught the flinch in his eyes.

Jaef's face flushed and his nose wrinkled. As he opened his mouth, another voice interrupted.

"Everybody stay cool. You know how much the metal merchant likes watching us fight. Don't give him the pleasure." Asher always seemed to be the voice of reason, amongst his friends as well as his enemies.

I walked past Jaef, but Asher didn't follow.

At least Jaef had shut up. I took a deep breath when I felt a tug on my arm, and I stumbled back, but Asher's voice soothed the anger brewing in my gut.

"From now on, crawl by the rules, or I'll string you up by the balls."

For a bare moment, Jaef held Asher's stare. I was certain Jaef wouldn't back down to the likes of Asher, but there must have been something in Asher's eyes that frightened Jaef. But Jaef played it off like Asher wasn't even a real threat.

"Sure thing, *Ash*," Jaef said, putting the accent on the last word. "Just make sure you and your girlfriend watch your backs. Crawling can be a dangerous job. Not that you would know, farmhand."

"He's not my boyfriend."

I saw Asher flinch, and then he nodded in agreement. "Yeah, not that it's any of your business anyway."

But Jaef had already stepped past us both, the side of his cart slamming into my shin as he went. The metal merchant shook his head and began weighing Jaef's haul.

"Let's go home, troublemaker."

I smiled at Asher and walked away from the line. But just before we got out of earshot, Jaef yelled at us.

"I'm going to eat like a king with all the rations I get from this haul!"

I paused, my body stiffened, but I didn't turn around to look at them.

"He's not worth the trouble."

"I know." I looked at Asher and then it hit me. "What you're doing up here?"

"Today is my rest day. Had nothing else to do and you seemed upset so I followed you. I wanted to make sure you didn't do anything stupid to the metal merchant."

Before I could tell him that I didn't need a babysitter, Asher looked at my cart and then at the road leading down to the village.

"Will you give me a ride?"

"We're a bit old for that, aren't we?" I tried playing it off like a mature woman, but the truth was that riding the cart down the hill with Asher on the back sounded wonderful.

"Yeah, you're right."

Before I could stop him, Asher turned and started walking down the hill. For some reason, I couldn't quite get myself to hop on the cart and speed down the hill past him.

3

J kept my distance, staying about fifteen feet behind him. I had to constantly grip the rope, too, as my cart wanted to speed down the hill without me, making me regret my decision to walk it down instead of ride it.

By the time Asher reached the village, the sun had dropped beneath a sky emblazoned with hues of scarlet and amethyst. The hill sloped away beneath us and the pot-holed road leveled out toward the clustering disarray of old huts and makeshift dwellings that made up our Hydran village.

The new autumn air chilled my skin, and I slowed my pace to pull my jacket tight. A few loose strands of hair concealed my face as I walked faster.

Asher slowed as if sensing my presence, and glanced over his shoulder at me.

"C'mon, slow-poke."

My fingers felt stiff, and a sudden wave of embarrassment made my stomach flip. He would never say so, but my grandfather was going to be so disappointed in the exchange from my haul.

"Rayna? You okay?"

Asher looked into my eyes for the first time since we'd left the gate. I threw him a fleeting smile.

"My hands are cold. Can't button my coat."

He reached his hands to mine. His skin felt rough and stony as he pushed my fingers aside and buttoned my coat from the bottom up. I lifted my chin and watched him as he buttoned the top one, stopping at my neck. He lifted his eyes to mine and smiled.

"Anything you want to talk about?"

I shook my head and mustered another unconvincing smile.

"Thanks," I said as I began to walk again.

He fell into step beside me, and we walked the rest of the way in silence.

The thing I liked most about Asher wasn't the way his thick brown hair gleamed gold in the sunlight or framed his carved jaw. It was that I could be in his company and not have to talk. I didn't have many friends like that.

Asher and I stopped on the broken pavement outside my home while a bunch of kids erupted from a nearby alley and ran through the streets, shouting and bickering over an old ball. I pulled my cart over the curb, fearful that those stupid kids would knock it over and trample my few pieces of rotting vegetables. I noticed Asher was combing through his backpack to produce a paper bag full of peas, a bunch of carrots, and two leeks.

"Here," he said, pushing his rations toward me.

I furiously shook my head and stepped back, flashing my palms. "Are you crazy? I can't take your rations, Asher…"

His full lips curved into a grin and he pushed them back at me.

"Sure you can. You're taking care of your sick grandfather. You need them more than me."

I clutched at the food rations and conceded with a heavy sigh, dropping my eyes to the crumbled pavement at my feet.

"You don't have to—"

"I want to. Take them."

He spoke with a raw and unchecked tone, and suddenly his hands cupped my chin. He raised my face until his eyes met mine.

I closed my eyes and felt his soft lips brush against my forehead. Asher's fingers trailed across the back of my neck, his fingers toying with wisps of my hair as he pressed his forehead against mine. The sound of the noisy kids and their shrieking mothers faded away as I felt him pull me closer.

I pushed away abruptly then, swallowing hard and biting down on my lip. I opened my eyes and saw his face red and twisted, his eyes looking off into the distance.

What was that all about?

I kicked at the gravel. "You'd better get home. It'll be dark soon enough."

Asher stepped back and dug his hands into his pockets.

"Yeah, definitely."

I nodded. My heart pounded in my ears, and I felt a tingle in my stomach.

A door creaked on rusty hinges, and I turned to see the light coming from inside of my home. My grandfather appeared in the doorway as a dark silhouette.

"Is that you, Rayna?"

When I turned to say goodbye to Asher, I saw that he was already gone.

4

I closed the door gently behind me and leaned against the flimsy timber while I worked to untie my laces. My boots hit the wall with an unsuccessful toss toward the wooden bucket which I kept by the door for such items. I shrugged and glanced at the rocking chair where my grandfather sat. He appeared to be settling down for a nap by the fire after letting me in.

"Asher walk you home?"

"Yeah, Pops."

I felt a cold draft and turned to see a new hole had formed about five feet up on the wall near the front window. We only had four rooms in total, and the single layer of crumbling brick and moldy plaster seemed to deteriorate by the day. My grandfather had told me about "indoor plumbing" and "the electric company" from when he'd been a kid, but those things were so far into the past that most of us had a hard time believing they'd ever existed in the first place. And we had a big fireplace and a stack of wood outside which was more than many other Hydrans had.

"I had to leave the fields early. My damn ankle is acting up again."

My grandfather had been sick, but he was too proud to tell me what it was. Some days he seemed perfectly normal and moved with the energy of a man half his age. And yet, on other days, he could barely get out of his chair. I would make him a cup of what he called his "magic tea," and that would put him in a better mood, but I noticed that it didn't seem to be as effective as it used to be.

"You shouldn't be in the village after dark."

"I know."

"And don't you roll your eyes at me."

I smiled, always fascinated with what my old grandfather could notice with his worsening vision and ailing body.

"Sorry."

He removed the wool beanie from his shiny bald head and his faded eyes crinkled with a smile.

"Do you know what I like about the dark?" His voice cracked, and he coughed a little.

"In the dark is great silence." I'd spoken the words with a metered cadence which prompted the question that always followed that one.

"And what will you find in the great silence?"

"What I choose to seek."

The other elders in the village called my grandfather by his first name, Howell. He was one of the few remaining survivors from the time before the world began to change and the city lights dimmed for good. Some of his friends had died off, and others had become too feeble to remember, but my grandfather had always been rich with stories and anecdotes—from cryptic messages I couldn't understand to wondrous tales about his youthful days.

A man of many talents, he had won the annual bow and arrow contest for seven years straight. My grandfather secretly taught me how to shoot, and now I could hit a running rabbit at twenty-five yards.

In his time, he was the best Crawler in the Hydran village. The villagers would look at him with silent respect as he'd walk through the streets with an air of certainty about the hidden tunnels of the lake and a cart filled to the top with his daily haul. My grandfather took care of me, and our home was the direct result of his hard work, even though the house had started to crumble over the years.

Aluminum stuck to the bottom of Lake Union in an almost endless supply in those long, lost decades. The hacks and the Hydrans posing as Crawlers would scavenge that, but only the best and most fit would risk the unpredictable passageways under the city in search of the most bountiful loot. My grandfather wasn't just one of those Crawlers—he was the best one, and the first to discover those secret passages.

With age, so too came the inevitable decline of his body. His crawling days passed, and he should have been enjoying the remainder of his time resting, reminiscing, and concocting wild yarns by the fire in his rocking chair.

But Corvis had changed the rules when he had first risen to power, in a time before my birth. He'd declared that Crawlers who couldn't dive anymore had to serve ten mandatory years working the fields to grow and harvest the bulk of the food for the Nest. In reality, hardly any of the old Crawlers lived five years after they stopped scavenging the lake. The whole system felt rigged because nothing grew anymore without what they called fertilizer, and that was another resource hoarded by the Crows and doled out when they felt it was warranted.

"You want some magic tea before I fix dinner? I'm going to make a nice soup to warm you up, and I'll boil you some water to wash up afterward. I picked fresh lavender to scent the water just the way you like..."

My voice trailed away as I glimpsed him again from my

kneeled position in front of the fireplace. His head had tilted to the side, his white-bearded chin pointed at me and his eyelids closed. His breathing rustled, and a snore ripped from his nose.

He opened his eyes suddenly and looked up at me with a sloppy grin. "I'm awake," he said, squinting as he moved his hand to grasp mine.

"I'll get you some medicine."

He nodded. "Just a little. We're almost out."

"It's okay, Pop. I'll crawl tomorrow and get more. I promise."

His eyes wandered to someplace beyond me and his eyes filled with tears.

"You're so good to me. You're a dream. A beautiful dream."

His mouth moved, but no more words came out. I recognized the daze settling over my grandpa, these episodes happening more often than they used to.

"I'll go fix us something to eat."

I dashed from the room before he could see the tears running down my cheeks, although his eyes had already closed and he'd started snoring again.

5

The cloudy water gripped my body like a cold vice as I kicked toward the surface for air. My lungs burned, and the chemicals in the water had begun to turn my skin white, a sure sign that I'd need to get out soon. I shut my eyes as my head broke the surface, gasping for air and checking the shore to make sure nobody had come to spy on me to find my secret dive spots.

I pushed my goggles up to my forehead, the water burning my face while the wind coming off the Sound numbed my nose. I paddled and spun around, again checking to make sure I wasn't being watched.

I'd left the house early when shades of orange and pink had smeared the sky, finding the lake spread flat and barren before me; only now was it the time when the farmhands would be heading to the fields and Crawlers would be arriving on the shore's cold sands.

Sleep hadn't come the night before, and I hadn't been able to crush the incessant thoughts circling through my mind. I had laid on my old foam mattress, staring up at the faint moonlight seeping between the cracks in the roof, and wondered as I had a thousand times before if things would ever change. After flopping around for a few hours, I'd decided to head to the lake and get an early start on the day's crawling.

My grandfather used to tell me that life is a continuity of change. He said everything is always changing, even when we think it's not. I'd wished for change, yet the stale stench and the despondency of our deprived village remained. And so did the Crows.

With all my heart, I'd wished my grandfather would get better. His illness was a change, yes, but a change I couldn't possibly see as positive—for either of us. The herb that relieved some of his sufferings and helped to clear his head for long stretches was not one easily found in the forest, and so I had to rely on trading with the metal merchant for it. And that could only happen once I had a big enough haul to cover our most meager food rations.

So far, though, this day was looking better than the one before, and I'd filled my bag with a few cans and some foil scrap I'd found wedged beneath a rusted car hood. The water currents pushed garbage into Salmon Bay from the Pacific and then down the Freemont Cut to our lake. Some of the Crawlers had gone out into Shilshole or Eliott Bay, but the closer you got to the Strait, the more dangerous the waters became. There wasn't just wreckage from the old world beneath the surface out there, but massive creatures that spawned for generations without the threat of humans—some of them big enough to pull a man under until he drowned.

As I stumbled up on the shore, I shook my bag—half-full, but not nearly enough to exchange for food and medicine. I needed more. I twisted around and scanned the shoreline to the west, deciding which of my secret dive spots I should try next.

A few boats drifted across the water, their sails a patchwork of old nylon and scrapped cotton. Some of the retired Crawlers cobbled together those makeshift boats to float on the lake and charge us working Crawlers to ferry our hauls to shore, and some of them lived on their boats. Although they could be odd, and occasionally dangerous, sometimes the hauls were too big to get to the shore in a bag, and you'd have to cut them in on a job. I'd long known which ones to deal with and which ones to avoid, but it was always a risk.

I looked past the boats and scanned the area near the old marina. I hadn't crawled that area for some time, the pickings mostly having been scavenged back in my grandfather's day. The underwater graveyards had once been a Crawler's dream, with sunken yachts and sailboats from long ago. Crawlers rarely bothered to search the marinas these days, yet I knew the heavy, submerged boats would shift every now and then, and sometimes that motion would loosen debris.

Sliding my goggles back down and taking a deep breath before biting my snorkel pipe, I slid back into the water, but stayed just under the surface. This allowed me to get a quick look into the submerged ruins but also to keep one eye on the boats—and the shoreline.

I used my feet to propel my body while keeping my arms extended while my tethered bag floated behind me. Not the best technique, but my legs were so strong that I could move through the water almost like a duck, paddling my feet below the surface. My skin lost even more color, and I knew that the longer I swam, the more chance I took of taking ill. My grandfather's generation had created thousands of synthetic chemicals and substances, and the city of Seattle had been home to millions. Whatever toxicity remained had contaminated the fields and then no doubt found its way to the low point—the bottom of Lake Union. There wasn't anything to be done about it now, and Crawlers considered it a risk they had to take.

My grandfather used to say that the greatest silence could be found in those underwater tunnels and passageways. Sometimes it soothed me, and at other times it frightened me. The darkness beneath the surface could embrace you like a cloak of ink, and even my Bright couldn't always penetrate those eerie, black tunnels. Before everything changed, many of those tunnels were surface-level streets, and the water had been unable to wash it all away. It wasn't unusual to come across the remains of a village roadway, frozen in time and sealed in the cold grave of the lake.

Only the best Crawlers dared to enter places like this even though their locations were widely known by many of us. I had never shied away from the challenge of the dangerous passageways, for the greatest reward belonged to those who were willing to take the greatest risk. But these days, exposed aluminum had become sparse, and I'd been forced to swim deeper into the black passages to score a bounty worth dropping before the metal merchant.

I dove, scoured, and sifted—poking under yacht hulls and massive rudders covered with years of crustaceans. Something glimmered from beneath an overturned beam near a sailboat. I yanked my bag to my side and pulled out my spade, using it to dig out around the beam. Chunks of rotten wood flaked off and floated around me until I'd scraped enough away to get my Band on it. The last thing I wanted to do was waste time and energy on a piece of scrap made of stainless steel.

The Band didn't stick to the scrap metal. I smiled and then used my shovel to dig deeper around the object. My lungs burned, and my head began to throb. I would need to go up for air soon. I dug out the aluminum and shoved it into my bag before kicking my legs and using my arms to help me back to the surface. Once there, I'd take a break on the shore before crawling again.

As I broke the surface, I heard someone yelling. At first, I thought the sound was in my head. It's been known to happen after spending too much time underwater. But the screaming grew louder, accompanied by the sound of splashing water.

I slid my goggles from my eyes and whirled around, searching for the source of the wild screams. Then I saw him—a boy. He flailed in the water about fifty feet away, his arms slapping at the surface while his desperate voice reverberated over the empty marina.

"Hold on!"

He didn't seem to hear me as his head disappeared beneath the surface. I kicked my legs and swam as fast as I could right at him. I reached the spot where I'd last seen him, slipped on my goggles, and dove straight down, madly scanning the murky water for signs of him.

My heart beat in my ears. I dove deeper, pushing through the water, my head filled with a strange contradiction. I needed to crawl, and yet, I couldn't let a child drown.

Where was he?

When I spotted his slight frame on the lake bed, I didn't waste a second. I moved through that water like a sleek fish, propelled downward until I reached him. His hair floated around his face in a dark halo, the long lashes on his closed eyes brushed against his sharp cheekbones.

And he wasn't moving.

I closed in on him and reached beneath his armpits, immediately dragging his motionless body up through the water. When we broke the surface, I gasped and clawed through the water while kicking my legs as hard as I could. I dragged the boy's lifeless body to shore.

As I staggered up on the sand, I collapsed beside him, panting and spitting while I looked the boy over. I noticed the slight rise and fall of his chest, and a wave of relief washed over me. He was alive.

I leaned closer to get a better look at his face, and that was when I realized I hadn't ever seen this boy before. I knew almost everyone in my village, and I knew he didn't live there. That's when I saw the permanent mark on his face, and my heart nearly stopped beating. The black smear on his pale skin was evidence enough.

He was Crow. And from the looks of it, he'd been punished for something.

The boy's eyes flew open beneath thick brows, and he peered up at me as his blue-tinged lips quivered.

"You almost got yourself drowned. And you nearly took me with you."

He said nothing, but sat up on his elbows, using his heels to push himself back along the sand and lengthening the distance between us.

"Hey, hey. Easy. I'm not going to hurt you, especially after I just saved your life." I smiled at him, pushing my hair from my face.

His black eyes sparkled, flittering between me and the trees behind us, his chest heaving as his deprived lungs drew in more air. He shrieked and then leaped to his feet.

"Wait!"

But he'd sprung to his feet and started running off like a jackrabbit, his soggy, brown jacket flapping behind him as he ran towards the forest.

I rose to my feet as he reached the tree line about a hundred yards away, turning there to give me a fleeting glance. Our eyes met briefly, and my lips curved into a waning smile before he vanished into the shadowed canopy.

I stood there alone, my feet anchored into the sand, and I must have stared at the tree line for longer than I'd realized, because when my mind cleared, and I finally moved again, the sun had reached its zenith and I knew I had to get back to the village.

---

*a*fter returning home, I dumped my diving gear and washed up as fast as I could, pulling on black jeans, a sweater, and my boots before yanking a comb through my tangled hair. I needed some time to hang with my friends at the Troll, unwind from a long day of crawling, and try to take my mind off of that bizarre kid I'd pulled out of the lake. What was that mark on his face? I'd have to remember to ask around, although something told me to be careful and only mention him to the people I trusted.

I walked through the streets of the village as kids ran by. The aroma of cooked beans and roasted venison made my stomach rumble, and I thought again about the lousy exchange I'd gotten from the metal merchant. Some of the families in the village had five or six kids. They needed more food, but they had more Crawlers, as well. I guess it all evened out in the end.

The main road from the village wound around to a rusted fence. I bent down and climbed through the hole in the chain link, which must've been there for years. All the kids knew about the Troll, but they also understood that, if you weren't old enough, you'd get your butt kicked. I'd been hanging out there for a few years. It was nice to escape from my main job of crawling, and from my second job as my grandfather's caretaker. I loved him more than anything, but the older he got, the harder it was to take care of him.

As I ducked beneath the roadway and slid down the gravel hill, I saw Asher perched on one of the Troll's massive knuckles, the guy's voice echoing under the bridge's supports as he made fun of our friends' hauls in his usual good-natured way. Even though Asher was a farmhand, we let him hang out with us Crawlers anyway. Everyone knew he'd have been one of us if it hadn't been for his lung condition.

My friend, Silas, started yelling at Asher, but I could tell it was in a teasing tone, not in an angry one.

"I filled up my bag twice today. Now tell me who else could have done that?"

There was an eruption of squabbles and heckles among the group, and Lyra, who was the most playful of my friends, sneaked up behind Silas and snatched away the burning herb he'd held between his fingers.

"Now tell me who else could have done *that?*" Lyra repeated Silas' question with a smile on her face before she jutted her hip to the side and took a deep draw of the smoke.

Silas feigned astonishment, looking at his hand as if he had no idea where the smoke had gone. He chased after Lyra as she dashed away, peeking out from behind the Troll's toes while the rest of the group laughed at the spectacle.

Asher spotted me mid-laugh and gestured for me to sit next to him.

I waved to everyone and climbed up while Silas and Lyra looped around the Troll.

"You guys can argue all you want about the size of your hauls, but we all know Rayna is the best Crawler here," Asher said, a ring of pride tracing his voice.

The gang agreed with nods, and their debate fizzled as the

conversation turned to the quality of the herb they had passed around. When it got to me, I accepted the rolled butt and filled my lungs with the thick curl of smoke as I leaned back against the Troll's arm. After passing the smoke along, I put my head in Asher's lap, feeling his hand resting on my shoulder. I closed my eyes and listened to my friends jesting and laughing about nothing in particular.

I wanted to ask them about the boy in the lake, but I waited until Silas, Lyra, and the others left, until it was only Asher and me. I stared at him for a long moment, and he could read my face. He knew I wanted to talk about something.

"Okay, what is it?" Asher asked.

"What are you talking about?"

"Spit it out."

Sometimes, having a friend that knew you almost as well as you knew yourself was a pain in the ass. My chest rose as I drew a breath and hesitated. I looked at the Troll for some advice. He didn't have any.

"Rayna?"

"Okay, okay. I was crawling this morning at one of the toxic spots, near the old marina, and I saw a boy drowning. I thought I wasn't going to make it in time to… you know, save him…"

Asher just looked back at me, his brows raised as he waited for me to continue.

When I didn't, he said, "And?"

"And I'd never seen him before. He wasn't from the village. Wasn't one of us."

His mouth twisted, and he huffed. "Then who was he?"

I shrugged and squirmed a little against the cold surface of the Troll's knuckle, suddenly feeling uncomfortable with the look in Asher's eyes.

"I'm not sure."

"What did he look like?"

"Young, maybe fourteen. He had a smeared, black 'C' tattooed on his face."

Asher's face fell, his lips pursed into a thin line, and his large hands gripped both my arms.

"Rayna. That is the mark of a Corvax Crow. They're the lowest class of Crows. You shouldn't have gone near him because the Corvax is cursed."

I shrugged him off and sprang to my feet with a grimace.

"So, I should have let him drown?"

He stood up. "Better that than face the consequences if Sandor finds out."

"I didn't have time to think about it. He was drowning, Asher. I wasn't going to examine him before saving his life."

"You took a big risk. You know that, right?"

I whirled around and climbed off the Troll, stalking away. Asher followed me.

"Wait up, Rayna."

I stopped, scuffed my boots in the gravel, and slowly turned to wait for him. As he neared, he lifted his arm to swipe back a lock of hair, his father's Band almost blinding me as it caught the last rays of the sun. Asher's dad had given it to him before he'd died, when Asher was just a kid. He never took it off. Some Crawlers claim it's the most powerful magnet in the village.

"I don't need a lecture. Especially from you."

He laughed. "I just want you to be safe, that's all."

"Thanks, Mom."

Asher smiled, and we walked side-by-side back to the village. But I couldn't stop thinking about the kid—that Corvax Crow. Who was he, and what had he been doing there at the lake?

7

_____

"*M*ore tea?"

My grandfather nodded as I eased the hot water from the dull, dented kettle. The steam fogged up his spectacles as the fragrant, herbal scent filled the room. I had thrown a few extra logs on the fire even though we couldn't spare many. He'd complained about his toes becoming numb, and I'd long ago decided to make my grandfather as comfortable as possible, especially on a night when he seemed to be mentally alert. That wasn't always the case.

"Thanks, hon."

The kid. What Asher had said. Corvax Crows. All these thoughts had been swirling in my head like the watery milk I had added to my grandfather's tea. I couldn't stop thinking about that boy, wondering what he'd been doing there in the first place. I'd never seen a Crow before, especially not a Corvax Crow.

"Did I ever tell you what happened about, let's see, forty, fifty years back?"

I'd heard every single one of my grandfather's stories, but I knew that telling them gave him a sense of purpose and often put him in a better mood. Unless it was one of his extremely depressing ones, I pretended not to have heard it.

"About the end? What made our lives the way they are today?"

"Yeah, that's the one. I think it was more like fifty years ago."

He took a sip and leaned back in his rocking chair, the thin quilt sliding from his bony knees. I'd stitched that thing so many times I could have sworn it was made of nothing but thread.

"We always knew it could happen, but nobody would've predicted it."

He liked to begin with a hook—my grandfather, the natural born storyteller.

"I think it was early spring. No, wait. Late summer. Yeah, right before the weather turns cold and rainy in these parts. The electricity, the *grid* as they called it back then. It just stopped working. No lights. No heat. No nothing."

"Didn't they have firewood?"

"Yes. No. Sort of. It wasn't like that. We had pipes coming into our houses. You know, like ones that would carry water. Except they carried electricity and gasoline—things we used to keep our houses warm and the lights on."

His inaccuracies grew with each retelling, but I had learned not to interrupt or correct him because it would kill his flow. Instead, I'd nod and stare intently while my grandfather recalled a time that may or may not have existed as he remembered it.

On this night, his eyes sparkled in the light from the fireplace, and his voice had an edge to it, like the man I remembered from my childhood who'd protected and taken care of me. At least on this night, the slow degeneration of his faculties would be stalled.

"That must've made life so easy. I'll bet people didn't have any problems. Nothing to complain about."

"Oh, Rayna. You don't know how wrong you are. People complained about everything back then. We had these devices that allowed us to communicate with other people all over the world, and yet folks did nothing but complain with them. 'This politician is crooked. My sporting squad is better than yours.' You'd be shocked at how much people found to complain about."

I sat down and poured myself a cup of the tea and leaned in closer. "Tell me more."

"Like I said, the grid went down. We didn't realize how dependent we were on that damn thing, excuse my language. Our entire lives revolved around the electrical current delivered to our homes, our cars, even to our fingertips. It was a wonderful time to be alive—until it wasn't.

"It wasn't like the TV or the movies had showed it the way it really ended up happening. No humans turned into the walking dead eating brains. No super flu. No global volcanic eruption. Nope. Things just went... dark. To this day, I ain't never heard an explanation that made sense to me. Not that it matters now anyway."

I pulled my jacket up around my neck, feeling the draft creep through our hut and knowing that the next part of the story would make me feel even colder inside.

"Once everything went dark, people lashed out. Wars were fought, and many people died. Most. I'm not sure how many or where, as most of what I know came from folks who'd headed west, thinking for some reason that things would be better here. Hell, many of my friends headed east for the same reason. But it didn't matter. The darkness was everywhere, and within a few years, people didn't have the time or the energy to fight. They needed to spend every waking moment staying alive. No more fresh fruits from South America or jeans shipped in from China. No more flying cars."

"Grandpa!" Although I couldn't tell for certain, none of the old timers told stories about the auto carts from that time being able to fly. I thought he'd thrown that in just to see if I was paying attention. "That's not true. They didn't have flying cars back then."

"Well, they should have. They'd been promising them since *my* grandfather's days."

"What about Brights?"

"Yeah, some of the old tech survived. Some of it in use far longer than people ever thought. They're still finding LEDs that light up, bright as the north star. Of course, around here, the Crows seem to have ended up with most of the solar cells and other gadgets that lasted after the grid fell."

The flash in his eyes faded and he coughed. The milk in our tea had turned my stomach sour.

"I was a teenager then, not much younger than you are now. I remember the time before the Crows. Before the Nest."

The mention of the Nest brought my mind back to the boy in the lake. My grandfather seemed cognizant, and he'd already taken the story beyond the point where he'd usually stop. I decided to probe a bit.

"Why don't they ever come down to our village? What's behind the walls of the Nest?"

"Ain't nothing for a Crawler to be worrying about. Asking those kinds of questions brings not answers, but trouble."

"What about Corvax Crows? What's their story?"

My grandfather leaned forward, his voice dropping into a low, raspy whisper. "Cursed. You see one, you'll know it. Get as far away from them as you can if you do. Nothing else to be said about the Corvax."

He coughed again, and I could tell that whatever mental sharpness the tea had spurred in my grandfather this evening had begun to fade like the heat from the fireplace.

"The Crows wasn't always the way they are. At one time, they were just the group that was able to figure out how to wire the solar cells to batteries. They used to be kind. They used to share. Before they built the scrapyard, they even let Hydrans in the Nest."

"Seriously? What changed?"

"What doesn't? Nothing in this world stays the same, Rayna. Don't you ever forget that."

Once he started with his sweeping generalizations given as advice, I knew our conversation was coming to an end.

"Is that why the revolution started? Because the people of our village wanted change but the Crows wouldn't give it to us?"

"Enough." My grandfather coughed, the single word coming out like the bark of an old dog. "Talk of the uprising is nothing but false hopes and broken dreams. Your father had no choice but to join the revolution, and it cost him his life. And your mother hers."

"I wish I would've known them."

"So do I, hon. So do I."

I stood up and reached for a hunk of firewood sitting in the corner, covered in cobwebs. Then I heard the floor creak behind me as my grandfather's rocking chair legs rolled across the uneven floor.

"Did I ever tell you what happened about, let's see, thirty... forty years back?"

"No, Grandpa. But maybe tomorrow? It's getting late."

He nodded, and didn't put up much of a fight. The old man was snoring within minutes.

8

I couldn't help it. I told myself it was only because I'd scored some loot at the marina the day before, but I knew I was kidding myself. I couldn't subdue the urge to return to the marina for a chance at seeing the boy again. Asher had said he was Corvax. Cursed. I couldn't stop thinking about what that meant. Some of us knew more about life in the Nest than others. I was sure the farmhands in the fields loved to gossip like anyone else. But Crawlers, well, we were in a world of our own under the water, and certainly not talking about the Crows. I didn't know if it was the look in that kid's eye or the C on his cheek, but I had to find out more about him and why he wasn't in the Nest with the rest of his kind.

A few hours and a lot of rummaging through the pallid wrecks littering the lake bed later, and I'd filled my bag almost halfway, maybe more. Not bad for a morning's crawl.

With each ascension to the surface, I'd run a quick check along the shoreline and the stretch of trees for signs of him. But he was nowhere around, and I forced myself to push the idea from my mind. I mean, the boy had been stricken with fear at the sight of me, so I wouldn't blame him for not ever returning to these parts. And if he couldn't swim, how did he end up in the water?

The marina sat on the lake's edge, and the Nest sat atop old Queen Anne Hill. The boy must've snuck down here for a reason. Wouldn't he have known that the lake was no place for exploring if you weren't familiar with its muddy, green waters? Maybe he was daydreaming, lost in his thoughts, and then found himself at one of the lake's steep drop-offs, where he slipped in. All things I would want to ask the boy if I ever saw him again.

I'd just finished pulling on some scrap foil that was jammed under a rusty mast pole when a sudden cramp bit into my thigh. I winced as I fumbled through the debris clouding the water while attempting to rub out the muscle spasm, but it just wouldn't let go of my leg, and it hurt like hell.

Finally, the pain subsided into a dull ache, so I twisted back to the foil with a renewed sense of determination, yanking that thin piece of aluminum out just before another cramp stabbed me fast enough to knock the air from my lungs. The foil came loose and I tumbled backward, grabbed my bag, stuffed the foil inside, and swam to the surface. My head broke through the water spitting a mouthful of foul water and even fouler language as I clambered to the shore. I had been robbed before, so I made it a habit to stash my bag in the brambles until I was ready to head home.

I was sitting on the soggy bank massaging my leg and silently willing the pain into submission when I was struck by an eerie feeling. I paused as the hairs on the back of my neck prickled and the whistling birds fell unusually silent. I squinted and held my breath, turning to peer over one shoulder. There was no one there, yet it felt as if I were being watched.

I exhaled slowly, then spun around the other way as fast as I could, gasping when I saw the boy standing by the wooded maze of trees about ten yards away. His thin arm clung to a barky trunk as he peered out from behind it. His dark hair was brushed across his forehead—a stark contrast to his pasty face that had frozen into a startled expression.

For a split second, our eyes locked, and I dared not move for fear of frightening him off again. The corners of my mouth curved ever so slightly into a smile, the movement enough to send him running back into the forest.

I scrambled to my feet and, without thinking, charged him with a burn in my belly that made me forget the cramp in my leg. I hadn't considered exactly what I would do if I caught him, or if indeed he *was* cursed, and I'd somehow be harmed if I did. I didn't care, and I didn't really think about it. I just knew I couldn't let him get away again. I had to discover more about the mysterious boy who Asher had called a Corvax Crow.

I felt the thick, cool shade of the trees after entering the forest in pursuit of the boy, stopping as the sweat on my skin began to feel like ice. Ahead of me, I could see a narrow track that snaked through the undergrowth. And that's where I heard the faint snaps of twigs and branches coming from underfoot—from under the boy's foot, I was sure.

My feet moved swift and light along the marshy trail, while I climbed through the bushes like a sinuating serpent.

I heard him running and his slightly panicked breathing—he knew I was chasing him. I felt like I was getting closer when, suddenly, the forest fell silent again. I stopped in my tracks and listened, searching the heavy, thick branches dropping over me as I continued down the trail more slowly. I looked from tree to tree —not venturing off the path, but looking for evidence of where the boy might have gone. I was getting close to the forbidden line, the place in the forest where the monsters lived and ate curious children—the story we'd all heard growing up that came with a fear we hadn't yet outgrown.

Crickets chirped, and the birds resumed their calls. I stomped down with one foot as I leaned back against a tree and closed my eyes. I was an amazing Crawler, and I could spend more time underwater without a breath than any of my friends. But between the dive, the cramp, and now this chase, my lungs were burning and begging for a rest.

A few moments passed, and I had almost given up on finding the boy when I spotted him sprinting out from behind a tree and bolting off again.

"Wait!"

I ran after him, but then the trail turned and I lost sight of him. As I stumbled around the bend and past a boulder, I saw the flap of his jacket disappear into a tunnel concealed by a hairy mess of wild grass and vines.

I stopped, breathless yet alert. I stared at the darkened entrance to the tunnel, hearing the words of every adult in the village inside of my head.

"Stay out of the tunnels. Kids go in there and never come out."

I looked down and saw that I had wrung my knuckles white, my mouth now feeling as dry as the high desert to the east.

---

9

*A*s I drew closer to what looked like a menacing, black mouth, I forced down the lump in my throat with a hard swallow and tried not to listen to my thundering heart banging in my ears, or the rational voice inside of my head that warned me to return to the village.

But I couldn't turn away. Who was this boy? Why was he watching me, and what was he doing in that mysterious tunnel?

I reached through the tangle of vines, my hands shaking as if they'd become writhing snakes. A different flutter grew in my stomach, and I opened my eyes and stared into the void. The first thing I noticed was the sound of dripping water in the distance. I knew water, at least. I estimated that the tunnel stretched at least two hundred feet into the darkness, which meant this wasn't just a sinkhole or hiding spot—this tunnel went somewhere. At some point in the distant past, earth had been mounded on top of it, creating a passage through an artificial hill.

A stench ruffled a few strands of my hair that had dried while I was running. It smelled of feces and the toxic brew of chemicals at the bottom of the shallow ponds that Crawlers avoided. But if air was coming from inside the tunnel, it had to mean that there was an opening on the other end.

It was then that I remembered stashing my bag and gear on the shore before I'd run after the kid. I cursed myself for leaving my Bright behind, as well, especially now that I was in a situation where I could really have used it.

My eyes adjusted, and I began to see the ribs of corrugated metal that formed the sides of the tunnel. Although I hadn't spent much time in them, I recognized this as one of the sewer pipes that used to run beneath the ruins, taking the waste away but to God knew where. I never could quite understand how people lived in my grandfather's day. Water sought the lowest level. All that waste would end up somewhere, right?

"He went in. Which means he'll probably come out somewhere else."

Speaking the obvious didn't calm my nerves. It didn't make me feel better about stepping inside the tunnel and possibly getting lost forever.

I caught a slight, fuzzy gray blossom in the distance. It didn't move, like the boy was showing me a beacon, beckoning me inside.

I put one foot in front of the other, the muted tones of the forest fading behind me as the darkness called. Another push of rank air made me gag, but I kept walking. Within moments, it felt as though the tunnel walls had begun to shrink. I'd already put my hands out to keep them from crushing me when I realized it must've been my own imagination—because the walls weren't moving. I'd spent more hours underwater and in the dark than I could count, but this felt different. Foreign. Forbidden.

As I progressed deeper inside the earth, I realized that the gauzy light was not a beacon after all. It had filtered down from above, illuminating the bottom of the tunnel with a smoky haze that revealed the rungs of a rusted ladder cemented into the moldy brick wall at the end of the tunnel.

"Am I going up?"

I had to ask myself the question, although my hands and feet had already made the decision. I clenched my teeth as my hands gripped the cold, rusty rungs. My feet pushed me up, and I kept my eyes on the wall in front of me. Crawlers loved going down. Going up—not so much.

By the time I'd reached the top of the ladder at least fifty feet from the bottom of the tunnel, my legs felt like rubber, and my arms shook. I lifted my head into the bright, late-morning sunshine. The birdsong filled my ears, and the smell of pink peonies replaced the stench that had filled my nostrils below. The sky looked blue, perfect, without any trees obscuring the light clouds floating by. I poked my head up far enough to get a look around.

This was not my world.

I gave up my compulsion to stay hidden and climbed the rest of the way out of the tunnel. A wall stood three feet away, behind me. It had to have been twelve or fifteen feet tall—definitely too tall to climb. I turned and saw that I was standing in the middle of a sort of courtyard, an interior garden. The back of a house ran parallel to the wall, with two shorter fences running along each of the other two sides. Fountains of stone frogs and fish shot water into the air. Real fountains, real water. Pink and white flowers bordered a stone pathway that led to the back door of the house. The mortar of the white brick appeared clean, and every window pane still had glass in it.

Laughter snapped me from my thoughts. I dove behind a small bush, my mind trying to process everything I was seeing.

"Noontime tea!"

The woman's voice sounded so delicate, soothing. I almost wanted to follow it myself until I realized I was no longer in my village. I'd gone up. Way up. I looked again at the high wall and the manicured vines and ferns bordering the water fountains and flower beds.

I was in the Nest.

10

_M_y chest almost exploded as I smashed through the thick weave of vines, not stopping to look behind me even when I knew I was on safe ground and bolting through the forest toward the lake. I broke through the trees and spotted the shoreline and the marina, but still my feet wouldn't stop until I collapsed on the grainy earth beside the bitter-smelling, gray water of the lake.

I could barely draw a breath as I heaved, feeling my face flushing and wiping sweat from my brow with the back of my hand. I glanced skyward, past the ragged line cut into the sky by the scrapyard's fence. Higher, until I could see the top of the wall surrounding the Nest on Queen Anne Hill. I had been on the other side of that wall. Had any of the Crows seen me? Had any Hydrans seen me? The questions began to fill my head so quickly that I closed my eyes and laid back on the sand.

"Settle down," I told myself.

But what exactly had I seen? I'd been in a courtyard on the other side of the wall separating the Nest from the rest of the world. I hadn't been _inside_ the Nest, necessarily. Whether I was or not, though, was this something I could share with anyone else? There would be consequences for my actions, I could bet on that.

But only if I had been found out.

When I sat up and looked around, it appeared as though I hadn't. The boy hadn't seen me, and none of the Crawlers had seen me.

I stood up, and retrieved my bag from its hiding spot. That's when my stomach dropped, and I wanted nothing more than to be back under the water, pulling foil from the wreckage of the past. My bag was much lighter than it had been when I'd run off after the boy. Like, 100% lighter—it was empty except for my gear which had my mark and would be easily traced to the thief if stolen.

"Where'd ya go without your haul?"

Jaef and his friends sauntered out from behind hunks of concrete bordering the lake, remnants of buildings that used to sit on the shore.

"Must've been really important." Jaef raised an eyebrow.

"Buzz off. I was chasing a rabbit. When Crawlers steal other Crawlers' loot, one's got to find another way to get food."

Jaef looked around at the others, a wide grin splitting his face from ear to ear. He waved a single finger at me like a mother would a naughty child.

"How deep did you go?"

He knew. He'd either followed me or been in that tunnel himself. I decided that making him as guilty as I was could be my best shot at keeping this hidden from the Chief.

"Deep enough to wish I'd had my Bright. But you already knew that."

"Yep. We all seen you, Rayna. You ain't seen none of us going where we ain't supposed to be."

"You won't tell Sandor. The Chief has more important things to worry about."

"Yeah." Jaef's eyes twinkled as he tossed back his long hair and pointed his chin at me. "He does have more important things. Like keeping his Crawlers in the water and not on some forbidden trip into the Nest."

"I wasn't in the Nest."

"No, of course not. You took a nap in that disgusting tunnel, leaving all your loot and gear behind."

I grimaced, biting my bottom lip and looking around. Three of Jaef's crew had formed a circle around me, and there was nothing I could do to get out of it. They'd already taken my day's haul, and I wasn't about to give them a pound of my flesh, as well. I decided it was wise to swallow my anger and try not to provoke him further.

"You got my scrap. Now leave me the hell alone."

He nodded, and then looked around at the other guys. "Getting a little long in the afternoon, fellas. I think it's time we head back to the village."

As Jaef walked past, he made sure to kick a footfall of sand up and into my face. He paused, waiting, hoping I'd engage. It took all of my internal strength not to fight back.

"Bye, *Rayna*."

The emphasis he put on my name made my stomach curl.

I really had no idea what to do. I ran a few steps, then stopped. Turned around, and picked up my gear and my empty bag and started running again. Jaef would tell Sandor. I knew that. What I didn't know was when. He could blackmail me for days, maybe weeks, and I wasn't about to let him steal anymore of my hauls. Jaef's family had deep connections to Sandor, and some say Corvus as well. As much as I hated to admit it, his word would be taken over mine. If I was going to be punished for being inside the Nest, so be it. Rather than give him the sick satisfaction, I'd get to the Chief first and explain exactly what had happened. Maybe he'd go light on me because I honestly hadn't known where I was headed.

That would be the best I could hope for. That, and not disappointing my grandfather. But it was all predicated on me getting back to the village—and to Sandor—before Jaef.

I ran over the rocky beach and through the heavy underbrush as the thorns tore at my skin. I'd have to cut through the brambles with the boys taking the trail. I had to get back to the village before they did.

11

I was such a fool. How many times had I been told to keep to the lake, to stay in the water? A Crawler's job was to *crawl*. My grandfather had warned me. Asher had warned me. But I'd been too stubborn to listen, and now Jaef would make me pay.

At first, I simply gave up. Jaef and his family had too many political connections. That entitled brat had the run of the village and he knew it. But the more I thought about it, the more concerned I became. I was in *deep* trouble and so I decided that I had to at least try to rationalize with the idiot before he took great pleasure in ruining me.

Through the entire run back to the village, I chastised myself. The facts were hard to ignore. I'd gone up and into the Nest, and Jaef knew it.

Glancing in the direction of Sandor's house, I didn't see Jaef or his crew. Maybe he was messing with me? Maybe even a jerk like him wouldn't do something so low as rat me out for something I hadn't intended to do. I walked past a short row of huts and toward the fence where the fields edged up to the village. If anyone knew where Jaef was, it would be the younger Hydrans tending the small plot where we grew the leaves we smoked on the Troll. He'd be there at some point in the afternoon, if he hadn't already. I spied Silas drooling over some fresh green buds.

He shot me a wide grin and waved a hand to motion me closer. "Rayna! Come look at these buds."

I shook my head and smiled as I walked over and eyed the furry, purple-bruised smoking leaves he lovingly held between two fingers. For Silas and other Hydrans, growing smoke was one of the only ways they could exercise some control of their lives. Whether it was Sandor or Corvis, all of us seemed to be subservient to some authority or another.

"Looking good."

"Been adding a few extra ounces of wild grass cuttings to the soil. Giving it a little shot of nitrogen."

I raised my eyebrows as if I understood how that would make the leaf better. I didn't.

"You'll thank me when you're puffing away on this baby." He titled the stem of the plant at me. "Wanna whiff?"

"Yeah, sure... Nice. Say, you haven't seen Jaef around?"

"Nope. He usually stops by after he takes his haul to the metal merchant. That's when he seems to have enough rations to trade for the smoke."

Yeah. I felt sure he'd have a whole bunch more metal to trade today. Thief.

"Why do you ask? I thought you hated that guy."

"I just need to know if you saw him."

"Not lately. Saw him and his gang heading toward the lake earlier this morning. After you, like always. But no sign of him since then. Want me to say something to him if I see him? Tell him you're looking for him?"

"Nah. That's okay. Nothing important. Crawler business; you know."

This time, it was Silas' turn to raise his eyebrows and pretend he knew what I meant.

"Cool. See you at the Troll later?"

"Probably. See ya."

I walked through the village, scanning the streets and looking over Jaef's usual hangouts, but I didn't see him. After passing by Sandor's house one more time, I circled back around to my own. I had probably overreacted, which I tended to do at times. After all, if Jaef got me in trouble and banned from the lake, how would he know the best spots to crawl without me to lead him to them?

When I got home, my grandfather was sleeping in his room. The field supervisor had been dismissing him from duty frequently these days which was not a good sign. Old Crawlers who couldn't farm anymore tended to die within a few months of their final dismissal.

Grandpa had remembered to shut the door, but his snores rattled the few window panes left in our hut. I hoped he hadn't already laid down for the night, which he'd done more frequently in the past few months. I peeled off my ratty wetsuit and dressed in my usual black clothes, and I gave my hair a good tug as I tore through it with the old comb.

My fingers worked hard and fast as I coaxed a log of wood to life to warm the place in case Grandpa woke up. I was pulling on my boots when I heard the heavy thuds of someone approaching the front door, followed by a thunderous knock that shook the thin, crumbling walls. It didn't sound like Asher's. It didn't sound friendly.

"Yes?" I raised my voice while at the same time trying not to wake my grandfather.

No reply.

As another boom rattled the hut, I flicked my hair from my shoulders and walked to the door, turning the knob and opening it with my right hand. The man before me was dressed in a long, dark brown jacket and a matching wide-brimmed hat. Wiry wisps of gray hair scraped and bristled thick against his throat, and his speckled eyes peered out gravely from behind round spectacles.

I didn't know his name, but I knew he was one of the Chief's advisors.

"Chief Sandor wishes to see you."

He wasn't Corvis, but Sandor was the head of our village, which meant he could still make my life miserable if he wanted to. I couldn't remember ever saying more than a few words to the Chief since the time I'd been a little girl. The fact that he'd sent one of his men to bring me to him was not a good sign.

Jaef and his big, fat mouth.

12

*C*hief Sandor lived in the largest Hydran house, made from wood, stone, and chipped brick. Mold covered the slanted roof with wooden shingles, and dark-leafed ivy crawled down the thick pillars while bamboo wind chimes and twisted, wired candleholders dangled from the beams. He wasn't our first Chief, and I didn't know who'd built his home. Of course, the leader of the village *should* have the most stable house, but that didn't stop it from bothering me when I thought of the crumbling walls in my grandfather's place.

My feet dragged against the gravel as I followed Sandor's advisor. The afternoon breeze rattled the chimes, and I closed my eyes for a moment as it brought me back to my childhood. Sandor had the only musical wind chimes in the entire village, and I could remember hearing them as a little girl, playing in the fields. They'd always brought me hope with their soft, welcoming pitch. My grandfather had told me stories about the bone chimes of the Orient, and he believed my affinity for Sandor's came from my Japanese ancestry. Maybe that was true, or maybe the chimes just made me feel safe. But today, the sound made me anxious. Maybe Jaef had ratted me out?

The advisor opened the door and waved me inside, shutting it quickly behind me and almost hitting me in the rear. As I stepped into the room ahead, I looked around. A single candle burned on the table, casting shadows on the wall. I thought it was odd, given the full sun beaming down outside; it was a somewhat rare, bright day in our part of the world.

The Chief sat with his back to the doorway in a high-backed chair facing an open window. His short-cropped, white hair cast out a silvery reflection from the sun's rays, his ebony skin glistening with sweat.

I had expected a greeting, or at least for him to turn around. But he did neither. I drew a breath and listened to the sound of the wind chimes and the shuffling of the advisor's boots on the front porch.

I lowered my head in deference to the man and his position. "Chief Sandor, you wanted to see me?"

He didn't move, and I was unsure if he'd heard me.

"Chief—"

He lifted his right hand and turned his head. He glanced at the candle and then back, almost gazing through me. I shut my mouth and bit my bottom lip as I waited for him to say something.

"Rayna, do you know why Lord Corvus selected me as the leader of this village?" Sandor spun on the chair so that now he was facing me.

I watched his hand fall back down to his lap, taking it as my cue that he now wanted to hear from me.

"Because you're noble."

The words sounded wooden even before they left my mouth. Truth be told, I had no idea why Corvus had selected Sandor as our leader. I had still been a child when the Chief had become ruler of the Lowlands, and I hadn't given the subject a whole lot of thought.

The Chief raised his hand again, holding his dark gaze upon

me. He continued, the rich, smooth, words commanding my undivided attention.

"I have been given this honor because I am capable of maintaining law and order in this village. It is my duty to make sure that we uphold our responsibility to our leaders, our village, and each other. I must make sure that rules are fair. And that they are followed. By everyone."

When he spoke those last two words, I knew what was coming next.

He paused and gave me a long look, the whites of his eyes yellowing, and his broad, flattened nose flared. I tried not to squirm, but I couldn't keep my fingers from tangling in a bunch.

Sandor leaned toward me, and I could smell the bread and onions he'd eaten for his noontime meal. I closed my mouth and took one step back.

"Villagers are taught from the time they are children that the Nest is strictly forbidden. No Hydran is to approach a Crow, and under no circumstance should a Hydran ever find himself—or *herself*—inside the Nest. These are the rules that have been in place for decades, and the ones which I have promised Corvus that we'd abide by. Now, if one of our villagers was to break this rule, how might that reflect on me?"

"Not good. I totally—"

"It would call into question my integrity, wouldn't it?" Sandor interrupted me with a question that I realized he didn't want to be answered.

So, I waited.

"And if my word is not good with Corvus, then the entire community falls to pieces. Yes, we help tend the fields, but it is the Crows who give us the fertilizer. It is the Crows who have built the irrigation system. It is the Crows who breed the beasts of burden. Without them, we don't farm. And if we don't farm, we don't eat."

I dropped my eyes to my boots and studied the worn, peeling tips.

"What is your job?"

I looked up and could see in his eyes that now he wanted an answer. "Crawler."

"What does a Crawler do?"

"Crawl."

He sat back, and the beginnings of a smile formed at the corners of his mouth.

"Right. The Crows maintain our farming infrastructure with the scrap we bring them. And without that trade, we get no rations. You see, if we don't all do our jobs and follow the rules, everything falls apart."

"I'm sorry, Chief, it was an accident and as soon as I realized where I was, I turned and ran. It won't happen again."

He frowned, his wrinkles carving spidery pathways over his forehead.

"I know it won't happen again, because you are forbidden to crawl until I have decided otherwise."

My heart slammed against my rib cage, and my mouth went as dry as a bone.

"What? No, please don't. It's the only way I can take care of my grandfather; he needs food and medicine, and he's sick— Chief Sandor, please."

"All things you should have considered before jeopardizing your livelihood. You're a woman now, no longer a child."

I felt the rush of tears ready to spring from my eyes.

"Please. I need to crawl, it's who I am. I don't know how to be anything else. And what of my grandfather?"

"Things you should have considered before going on your *little adventure*. If word gets out that villagers can explore without consequence, then I have nothing but anarchy on my hands." The Chief turned away and shifted his gaze back to the single candle. "I've made my decision."

I could feel the heat burning in my chest, the rush reddening my face. I made fists with both hands and stood up straight, my chin out.

"Understood."

Sandor didn't bother to look at me again. Instead, he dismissed me with another wave of his right hand, and almost instantly the door opened, and sunlight flooded the room.

The advisor's eyes looked down with disdain, and now the chimes seemed to be mocking me. I walked across the threshold and had taken several more steps when I heard the door slam behind me. No point in pleading my case or even turning around.

I ran toward Freemont, past the children playing in the dirt and the women washing clothes near the lake. I couldn't even imagine what tomorrow morning would bring, when I wouldn't be either in the water or on the shore.

13

I peered up at the face of the Troll with a grimace and ignored the chatter of my friends in the background. I had been sitting crossed-legged and hunched for what seemed like an eternity. I couldn't think of anything else beyond what had happened, no matter how hard I tried. I shrugged and shifted my gaze back to the dirt at my feet. I would have rather been alone, but I couldn't go home and face my grandfather.

A bout of laughter rang out. I turned a cold shoulder on the commotion until the unmistakable guffaw of Jaef's laugh split my head like a migraine. I whirled around and saw him snickering, pointing at me as his friends high-fived each other.

"What time you crawling tomorrow, *Rayna?*"

As soon as Sandor had started talking, I'd known what that rat had done. What I still didn't know was how much Jaef had seen or what he'd told Sandor. Clearly, our village leader assumed I'd made it inside the Nest, and I wasn't naïve enough to cop to anything intentional. I'd taken my punishment while claiming it was accidental, which in a way, was the truth. But that didn't mean Sandor believed me. You didn't run the village without being able to manage and control people.

"I guess now you'll have to dive for your own puny hauls instead of stealing someone else's," I said.

His friends ooh'd and aw'd with a sing-songy tone as if trying to provoke both of us into a fight, even as my eyes narrowed, and a flash of red blinded me. I blinked a few times and spotted Asher out of the corner of my eye. He must have noticed the fury all over my face because he shook his head as if to tell me to let it go.

But I didn't care. Everyone hanging at the Troll knew the deal. I was the best Crawler in the village. Jaef was nothing but a hack. He'd gotten me out of the lake, and now he'd have to figure out how to match my productivity. Good luck with that.

I stood up and brushed the dirt from my pants, taking a few steps away from Jaef, toward Asher. That was when I felt the cold, slimy sensation on the back of my neck. The boys erupted in laughter.

Black Mud.

It was everywhere on the shore, and we did our best to avoid it. The stuff smelled like a dead rat, and it took weeks to wash the odor out of your clothes. When I put my hand on the back of my neck, I already knew who'd thrown a pile of it at me. The Black Mud ran down my back in cold rivulets and was all through my hair.

A roar started in my throat and exploded through my tightened jaw as I ran at Jaef as fast as I could. His eyes had gone wide, and his mouth formed a dark O as I bulldozed into him, tackling him to the ground.

The dirt billowed up around us as we wrestled each other. I used my legs to push my body on top of him. Even though he had fifty or sixty pounds on me, I was able to sit on his chest and keep his arms pinned beneath my legs. I didn't hesitate, slamming my fists into the side of his head. I could see my knuckles turning red from the blows, but I was too jacked to feel it. All sound faded away except the light whimpering coming from Jaef's throat.

I didn't realize it at the time, but Asher had grabbed me by the shoulders and tried pulling me off Jaef, but he couldn't do it. I had my knees firmly planted on the jerk's shoulders and my fists continued to fly.

"Rayna! Stop!"

It was probably a good thing Asher used my name because I think it broke me out of my spell long enough to make me pause and think about what I was doing. Jaef's crew had come down off the Troll, and now they were all pulling at me while my arms and legs thrashed.

Asher saved me. If I had continued beating on Jaef, he might have had to go see the village doctor—or worse. And there would be no way of hiding a black eye or a split lip. Luckily, Asher pulled me off Jaef before it was that bad.

"I'm fine."

But Asher knew I wasn't. He steered me away from Jaef, who was now climbing to his feet and wiping a trickle of blood from his right ear. The guy's friends looked from him to me, unsure whether they should shut up or come at me.

"You okay?"

"I said I'm fine!"

Asher would understand it was the adrenaline screaming at him, not me.

"You should go home." His voice sounded like a distant echo.

I started walking, and then turned around to look back at Asher. His mouth had twisted up in a silent frown, and he extended his hands to offer me a hug—as if I would do that after pummeling Jaef in front of his friends. Guys always thought girls need to be comforted. Sometimes, we just needed to be pissed.

"Yeah, home. Because nothing I do out here is going to make any difference."

Asher said something, and I think Jaef began to yell at me over top of him, but I ignored them both. At that moment, home didn't sound like enough. I wanted to run from the village and never come back.

14

"*R*ayna—wait up!"

Asher's voice mixed with the wind whirling in my ears as I ran along the edge of the lake. Blood was coursing through my system like hot steel and my heart ached from smashing against the inside of my rib cage, but I didn't stop. I didn't want to talk to Asher, or anyone else for that matter.

"Rayna!"

As I stole a glance over my shoulder, I noticed he was catching up to me, and I knew I had no chance of outrunning him and his long strides. Still, I had to try. I gritted my teeth and willed my legs to move more quickly while inwardly cursing my shorter frame. It wasn't the first time I'd resented my lack of height.

I wanted Asher to just go away and let me enjoy sulking all on my own. The fact that I had kept running should have been enough of a hint.

I heard his footsteps behind me, and then I could almost feel his fingers brushing at my back as he reached out. I twisted around with a scream and kicked out in anger. The dirty foam scum on top of the water covered his shirt, but it wasn't enough for me. I'd figured I'd have time to kick at the water again before he caught me.

I'd figured wrong.

Just as I reared my leg back to kick through the water once more, he crashed into me and we fell into the lake, with me cushioning his fall.

I grimaced as I tried to push him off of me. "Get off!"

Asher pushed up with his arms, but the bulk of his weight still pinned me beneath him. I glared up as the beginnings of a smile formed on his face, and he shook his head.

"Only if you promise not to run away," he said, brushing the strands of wet hair from my face.

I turned away and scowled before slamming my fists up into his chest. He barely flinched, but his brows raised.

"For God's sake. Do you always have to be so stubborn?"

I didn't answer.

"Promise me you won't run, or I'm not letting you up."

My eyes began to sting, and I nodded silently. I didn't have it in me anyway. I was pretty sure our collision had sapped any adrenaline that might've still lingered in me.

He stood up, and I took the hand he offered. Asher led me over the embankment and to a grass clearing where we sat in the afternoon sun, hoping the rays would eventually dry us off.

I focused on wringing out my hair and trying to subdue the tears threatening to burst, his unrelenting stare boring right through me.

"What happened?"

I shrugged and forced myself to look at him. His eyes shone tender, and my focus began to crack. Why did he have a knack for undoing me?

My fingers twisted and turned until I could no longer coax a drop of water from my dark strands. My hair might've mostly dried, but my tears were just getting started. They fell hot over my cheeks, and I looked away from him. My shoulders started to tremble then, and I quivered as I buried my face in my palms and shook my head.

I told him everything. I explained what had happened with the boy, the tunnel, what I had seen at the top of it, and my conversation with Sandor.

"Not at all?" he asked afterward.

"Nothing. I can't even be near the lake. Probably shouldn't even be here now."

Asher leaned back and let loose with a low whistle. "But it's all you know how to do?"

I nodded.

"And you're the best Crawler here. Everyone knows that. Even Jaef. Why do you think he's always messing with you? He's insecure, and he's jealous."

I nodded again, getting angry as I heard the situation spoken back to me and yet feeling oddly defiant in wanting to prove Sandor wrong.

"Yes, Asher. Yes. I don't think the Chief left anything unclear. I don't need to hear it again from you."

"Sorry. I'm trying to wrap my head around this. What about your grandfather?"

"I'm not really sure how I'm going to take care of him. He's sick. The field supervisor has dismissed him every day this week."

He wrapped his arms around his legs and brought his knees up to his chin, reminding me of the little boy I used to run through the alleys with not that long ago. What I wouldn't have given to go back to that simpler time. The older I got, the more confusing things became.

"I'll help."

"I can't ask you to—"

"You're not asking me, and I'm not waiting for your permission. I will help get you and your grandfather rations and medicine, even if I have to steal it."

"If Jaef or Sandor find—"

"They won't."

"What about your family? Rations for your mom?"

"I'm telling you, Rayna. I can help. Stop being a mule and just accept it."

My swollen eyes clouded hazy with the remnants of tears as I gazed at the water glittering in the sunlight. My chest rose, and I sighed so heavily.

"Okay."

He smiled and reached for me. I leaned my head against his chest and inhaled his scent, listening to the drum of his heart. He wrapped his arms around me, and for a moment I enjoyed the calming, safe warmth of his embrace.

I lifted my chin and shot him a quick smile. "Thank you." Then I snaked my arms around him and pulled him closer while squeezing my eyes shut.

15

Grandpa's whiskers scratched against my cheek as I bent down to give him a kiss. His hands, wrinkled and blotched, clutched at the old quilt as he tugged it up under his chin and he gave me a wistful smile. I sat in the wooden chair beside him and handed him a hot mug of his freshly-brewed herbal medicine.

"Here, drink up."

He looked at me, his eyes fading as he struggled to focus. He frowned then, and his gaze fell on the mug I offered.

"Ah, yes, thank you, hon." His reddened fingertips reached for the mug.

It was getting harder and harder to hear him lately, and I had to strain to catch most of his words. He had run out of holes on his leather belt, and his skin appeared thin, almost translucent.

I held my breath while bracing myself. My guilt was eating holes in my stomach, and I needed to tell Grandpa about what had happened. When I wasn't heading to the lake in the morning, he'd want to know why.

"I'm sorry," I said.

He slurped at the tea before resting the mug in his lap. I

wasn't sure if it was too hot or if he didn't want the tea but was being polite, pretending to sip it.

"Guilt is a wasted emotion. What have you to be sorry about?"

I looked beyond him and studied the cracks in the walls, shivering with the cool night air leaking through them. What did I have to be sorry about? How about this damn hovel for a start? Or the lack of food, or the rickety rocking chair barely holding his weight? How about everything? But I couldn't get into all of that—my news would be more than enough to shatter him.

I dropped my eyes to the quilt and began to bunch the flimsy fabric between my fingers. "I'm not allowed to crawl. Sandor has forbidden me until further notice."

My grandfather looked at me with his mouth open, but no words came out. His sagging, weathered face twisted as his brain processed what I'd said. I'm sure it made no sense to him why the best Crawler in the village would be off the job. I wasn't thrilled about getting into that conversation.

I chewed on my bottom lip, waiting for a response. Surely, I had brought shame to the family and to him. Grandpa had never been forbidden from crawling in his days.

"Grandpa? Did you hear me? I can't crawl for aluminum anymore—you know what that means, right?"

"I know what that means." His voice firmed, more so than I'd heard for some time.

I glanced at him, my eyes down and my hair falling around my face. This felt worse than being lectured at by Sandor or made fun of by Jaef. I was inflicting pain upon the man who had raised me and taken care of me through most of my life. I watched an ant run along the sagging floor and disappear through a gaping hole.

"I'm sorry."

He rubbed the top of my head with a knobby hand. I hid my grimace and grabbed his hand for a squeeze. His fingers felt calloused and cold, and I tucked his hand underneath the quilt.

"I'm not angry. But what happened? He catch wind of one of your rebellious streaks?"

I stood up and looked down into his eyes. How did he know?

"Why would you say that?"

His melancholy smile blossomed slowly on his face. "Because you're just like your father. He could never follow the rules, always doing things his own way, questioning authority at every opportunity."

"Well, in my defense, I really didn't know where the tunnel would lead me. I was only—"

"Tunnel? Please tell me you weren't in *that* one. The one with the ladder at the end?"

I nodded.

"Oh, Rayna. You're not a kid anymore. You know the rules of the village. You, better than anyone, should know where you can dive and where you can't. And you absolutely know you can't be anywhere near the Nest. Ever."

I shrugged. "I was looking for this boy, some kid with a C on his face. He was drowning, and I wasn't about to let him die. When he ran off, I chased him and, before I knew it..."

"Before you knew it, you were headed for the Nest and breaking the rules." He paused, and I thought my scolding was over. It wasn't. "He must've been a Corvax Crow. They're cursed. What were you thinking?"

I guessed I hadn't been. I'd always been impulsive, and it was what others said they liked about me. Maybe it had been cute when I was a kid, too, but now, not so much.

Grandpa looked up at me, and I gulped. Nothing felt worse than disappointing him. He deserved better, and I couldn't keep the growing resentment for Jaef from burning inside me like a ravaging fever. If he had just kept his damn mouth shut...

"I wasn't thinking," I said after another moment. "And now, I can't get us food or medicine."

"We'll get by somehow. We always do."

Grandpa was already a bit weird on Asher even though I had to remind him that I wasn't ten years old anymore, that I could handle relationships all on my own. Either way, bringing up my friend now and what he offered didn't feel right, and it would only get Grandpa riled up again. At this point, I would be relieved when he ran out of energy and turned in for the night.

"The rules are important. They're in place for a good reason, and you must obey them. Promise me."

I nodded, but inside I could feel my stomach twisting. Why? Why should we continue to accept Sandor's rules because some Crow atop the Needle said so? Why were we down here, diving in the filthy water and risking our lives for metal that got hoarded and used by people living in the Nest? And *what* did they have in there?

I wasn't sure why the rush of emotion and such a barrage of questions came at me then, while having a simple conversation with my grandfather, but the levee had broken, and I couldn't hold the floodwaters back.

When I'd think about it later, I'd realize that was probably the moment when things began to turn.

Grandpa must have taken my silence as disobedience because he launched into what, for him, was a rare lecture.

"You listen to me, young lady, and you listen well. Breaking the rules will bring chaos and death. Your father died in the uprising, and your mother also paid with her life."

The uprising was certainly not something I wanted to think about. That act of senseless violence took both of my parents from me. I wasn't about to listen to the virtues of Crow law, especially from my grandfather.

"I'll obey."

"I'm not convinced, but I will take you at your word. Corvus and the power of his office are not to be trifled with. Things could be worse, girl. *Much* worse. We have food, water, fire, and a roof over our heads. I've seen other places in my day, and we're a few of the lucky ones. All Hydrans have a responsibility to maintain order by following the rules, and Sandor is there to make sure that happens. You can't change what you did. But you *can* decide what you're going to do now."

"I know. I will."

"Will what?"

"I'll follow the *rules*."

He grimaced at my drawn-out enunciation of the last word, as if the sarcastic bile had risen in his own throat.

"Go to work. Do your job—whatever Sandor decides it's going to be from now on. That's how responsible adults act. They don't run around chasing cursed children or thumbing their nose at laws that have been on the books for generations. It's time to grow up."

I fought back the tears, unable to remember a time when Grandpa had spoken like this to me.

I couldn't speak, so I nodded and tapped him lightly on the shoulder as if to reassure him that I would be a good girl. I walked to my bed after that, and let Grandpa handle his own nighttime ritual.

Staring at the ceiling, I began to think. Rule followers never changed the world. Nothing valuable was ever given to those who practiced blind obedience and compliance. Whether it was aluminum or freedom, life's valuable stuff had to be *taken*.

16

A rush of heat came into my room, tingling up my arm. I shot up, and my eyes darted around as I heard the first scream. An orange glow illuminated my room and sweat trickled down my forehead.

The first thought that came to me was Grandpa. I swung my feet over the side of the bed and rushed out of my room and into his.

His bed was empty.

I hurried into the living room and checked his chair. Like his bed, it was empty.

More screams came from the village. I ran outside to see what was going on.

I stepped like a ghost through the hazy alleys, my lungs clogged thick with smoke. A moment of confusion lingered as I gazed around, my eyes burning from raining ash while desolation marked the night sky with a soaring blood-orange glow.

Fear gripped me like an unrelenting vice, and I stood still with the realization that my village had burned, becoming charred with the raging flames of damnation. My hands trembled uncontrollably as I tried to make sense of what I was seeing.

Bodies lay sprawled all over the village. Hydran corpses left for dead by the ones who'd ambushed our village.

But it wasn't the bodies that made me shake—it was the heads of villagers sitting atop spikes.

Mothers and fathers clutched their children and covered their eyes as they fled from their scorched homes. My eyes scanned the rows of severed heads, seeing the familiar faces of my fellow Hydrans. Crawlers I'd dived with since we'd been kids. Men and women I'd known my entire life. Even children hadn't been spared from decapitation and spectacle.

My body went numb when I saw the head at the end of the row. My weak legs barely got me over to it, and I dropped to my knees in front of the spike.

"Grandpa?"

His purple and black tongue hung from his mouth, and his pale eyes stared at nothing. I reached up and touched his cold face. Ran my hands through his bloodstained hair. Squeezing my eyes shut, I bowed my head, and the tears flowed.

It wasn't until I heard the macabre laugh coming from behind me that I raised my head. I slowly turned to look over my shoulder.

Corvus. I had only seen the man in paintings, his beady eyes and pointed nose both red and splotchy. And yet, I knew it was him before me.

His laughing only grew louder as the fire rose behind him, lighting the sky.

"No." I shook my head. "No, this can't be."

Corvus stared at me and narrowed his eyes. A grin stretched across his worn face.

"No!"

SWEAT BATHED MY BROW, my nightshirt already soaked through as I sat upright in bed. I shivered as the cool air prickled against my damp skin. My hands trembled while I heaved, and my eyes darted wildly in the dawn light.

It was only a dream, a nightmare, I told myself while I tried to quell the rising nausea.

I didn't have the luxury of the mystical. Not many in the village had. Our lives had been filled with arduous work and meager entertainment, so it wasn't until old age when Hydrans began to think of things beyond our earthly realm.

That's probably why the dream had hit me so hard. I didn't know what to do with it or how to react. As a kid, I hadn't remembered many dreams—even after I'd lost my parents. Some mornings, I'd wake up and feel as though I'd been crawling all night, but my muscles wouldn't be sore.

Sometimes I'd wake up with a headache and know that my mind had been pushed to its limit while I slept, but again, I could rarely recall why.

This dream. This was different. Without trying to sound like one of the crazies who lived out in the ruins, I had to admit that it had felt like a vision. *No... A warning.*

As my breathing slowed, I began to hear the sounds of morning in the village. Clanking pots and mothers yelling at children to go out and fetch the day's supply of water from the well. Dogs barking and roosters crowing.

It began to feel normal. But there would be no way for me to convince myself that that was true, no matter how long I laid upon my lumpy mattress, trying to lose myself in the familiar chaos of daybreak rituals.

My grandfather hadn't spoken much about dreams, but there were mornings when I knew he'd had them. And I was not about to ask him to explain them to me. I knew I could try to push my dream aside and bury it deep inside, but that wasn't going to work.

The Crows had come down from the Nest, en masse. They'd burnt my village to the ground and murdered everyone I cared about. Well, in my sleep. I'd never had a dream that was so vivid or realistic. Ever.

I sat up in bed and slumped back against the ancient headboard, the animals painted on it now chipped or faded into pale ghosts. I stared at the sagging ceiling as the first light crept pale and silver into the room, and I knew what I had to do next.

I would need to break the rules. Again. For the sake of my village, my grandfather, and all my friends, I needed to go through the tunnel and back to the Nest. If a storm was indeed coming, I would find out.

17

*C*areful not to wake Grandpa, I snuck into the kitchen to wrap some stale bread in a worn piece of cloth and refill my canteen with boiled water before stuffing the supplies into my bag.

As I splashed a few drops of water onto my face, I closed my eyes and thought about Grandpa's stern words from the night before. I knew what I was about to do would upset him, but the dream had seemed like a warning about the Crows, and something inside told me that I didn't have much time. I had a feeling that things in the Nest had begun to change, and it wouldn't take long for the negative energy to roll down Queen Anne Hill and into our village.

Flashes of burning corpses returned. I shook my head and blinked away the horrific dream as I twisted my dark hair into a braid. I didn't want to disappoint Grandpa again, but I couldn't stand by and do nothing after that nightmare. I couldn't ignore what the universe was showing me.

I crept to the front door and pulled on my boots, and then turned to look at the empty rocking chair.

"I'm sorry, Pops."

And I walked out the door.

The crisp, early morning air tingled the tip of my nose and my breath clouded in front of me. I walked briskly along the dirt path that wound to the lake while the village began to stir. Soft voices and pattering feet shuffled behind thin hut walls, while the wails of hungry babies and toddlers shrieked across the still village as I passed silently in the direction of the tunnel.

My mind was so busy with my task, and striking flashes of my burning village, that I marched ahead and tuned out my surroundings. It was only when I'd reached the outskirts of the village that I heard Asher's call. I stopped and looked at the sky, shaking my head before turning to face him.

"None of your business."

He rushed toward me with a lopsided grin, his hair falling over one eye. "Where are you going so early?"

I shook my head and gave him a light smile. "Nowhere. Turn around and go home."

Asher cocked his head to one side and then glanced in the direction of the tunnel. "Oh, no. You are not going *back*. You can't be that stupid."

I felt the heat rise in my cheeks, and I took a step closer to him. He put his hand on my shoulder and I knocked it off.

"If you ever call me stupid again, I'll break your nose."

He took a step back and put both hands up, palms out. "I'm sorry."

"No, you're not. That's just something people say after they act... *stupid*."

"You're risking your life. All our lives. Please, don't do this. Let's go somewhere we can talk and where you can cool down for a while."

"I've already been told I can't crawl anymore. I don't need you telling me what to do, as well. Now, get out of my way and leave me alone."

I brushed past Asher on my way to the tunnel.

"Rayna?"

I stopped and rolled my eyes, but I didn't look at him. "What?"

"I'm begging you. For once in your life, please don't make trouble where there isn't any. Just follow the damn rules, would you?"

I could hear him breathing, and I felt the heaviness in his words—but I had to do what I had to do. I turned around. His soft blue eyes sparkled as they met mine, and I almost lost my resolve.

"I'm going for a walk. I'll be back later."

He was silent, yet his eyes never left mine as the rising sun caught the crown of his hair like a golden halo. A glimmer of worry was etched on his face, and I could tell he was reluctant to walk away.

He sighed. "Can I come with you?"

"Not a chance."

"I knew you'd say that."

Hearing the tone in his voice, I turned all the way around to face him. He smiled, trying to draw me in, but I wasn't going to fall for it. "Go home, Asher. I don't want to hurt you, and I don't want you to get hurt."

His expression grew pale. "Rayna, please."

Shaking my head, I said, "Don't follow me."

With that, I walked away, not turning around again. Asher said nothing else, and he didn't follow me.

18

By the time I reached the mouth of the tunnel, the birds had stopped singing, and the trees seemed to be hovering just above my head. The morning dew coated the tall grasses, making them look like blades of glass in the new sun. The warm breeze had already begun to chase the night's chill away. I stopped in the middle of the path and stared at the cold, black, entrance to the tunnel.

I heard my grandfather's voice. I saw Asher's face. But I couldn't stop my feet from moving forward. I plodded ahead until I could smell the dank odor coming from within. Sandor would freak out if he knew I was standing there, contemplating going forward at all, when I knew deep down what I was going to do anyway.

I shifted my weight to one leg and chewed on my bottom lip as I moved the vines and peered into the tunnel. I wasn't really breaking the rules, going inside the tunnel. That's what I told myself. Climbing the ladder, though… Yeah, climbing the ladder was when shit would get real.

I peered at the faint light at the far end of the tunnel, where I knew the bottom rungs of the ladder plunged down through the ankle-deep water. I looked back at the path, unable to tell if Asher had listened to me. I couldn't see him, but that didn't mean he hadn't followed me. Either way, I felt the tunnel pulling me forward, and not even the talon-like branches of the tall pines could hold me back.

"Our secret," I said to the birds, or whoever else might be listening.

Before I could change my mind, I slid between the thick, ropy vines and slipped into the tunnel. As I crouched down and scampered along the concave side, I could feel sweat breaking out on my forehead. I stopped midway and twisted my fingers deep into my braid while trying to swallow the lump in my throat. My racing pulse throbbed in my ears.

"What are you doing?" I asked myself.

People would find out. Someone would tell Sandor. And then what? I wasn't just risking my own freedom. I was now putting my grandfather's health on the line. I stopped and looked over my shoulder. The morning sun and fragrant scent of pine tried luring me out of the darkness, and I took a step back before stopping again.

"No. I have to do this. I *can* do this."

Even though I had spoken the words, my legs had begun taking me in the other direction—out of the tunnel and toward the path leading to our village. I wanted to think my reluctance was about obedience or my grandfather, but I couldn't lie to myself. Inside, I knew I was afraid. Pure and simple fear was pulling me back.

Between my steps in the sloshing water on my way back to the path, I heard something. I stopped and stood still, convinced it was the tubular steel aqueduct playing tricks on my ears. And then I heard it again.

Singing. From the opposite end of the tunnel.

I leaned back against the cold, wet wall as a shiver ran down my neck. I held my breath, waiting for the song to pick up again. It did, the light melody carrying through the tunnel, floating above the rat-infested waters at my feet.

I hadn't noticed that my feet had spun, and my legs had moved me toward the ladder once again—toward the singing. Who would be down here? But later I'd think I had known the answer already, upon hearing the voice at all, and that's why I had unconsciously turned around.

His silhouette emerged through the gloom like a glowing apparition, and as he stopped fifteen feet in front of me, his mouth was open, but he was no longer singing. His eyebrows drew upward into an inverted V. I could smell the faint aroma of hazelnuts and bread. His hair had been combed, and his garments were clean outside of where they had brushed against the greasy rungs on his way down the ladder from the Nest above.

As I took another step forward, he spun around and sprinted for the ladder. I may not have been the fastest runner in the village, but I could definitely chase down a kid.

He was within five feet of the ladder when I reached out and grabbed him by the shoulder. "Stop running!"

The boy squirmed and tried throwing off my hand, so I grabbed him by both shoulders and pulled his face toward mine. "Just stop!"

He gave my shin a half-hearted kick with his leather boots before screeching at me like a rabbit in a snare.

"I'm not going to hurt you. I just want to talk."

His eyes flashed, and I could hear his teeth grinding. But then something clicked when he looked at my face.

"You're the girl."

"Yeah. I saved your ass. You're welcome."

I felt the muscles in his shoulders relax, and I let go. The boy took a step back and, even in the low light, I could see his lips brighten and a blushing rose hue darken his milky complexion.

"You shouldn't be here. It's against the rules."

The word rang in my head. *Rules*.

I chuckled to myself, feeling my face blush as I said the word my grandfather had been saying to me so many times lately.

I waited, but the boy only stood there, silent and still.

"I'm not going to hurt you," I said.

"I know."

He was Corvax. I knew this with full certainty. I should have turned around and walked out. But just because you can do something doesn't mean you should.

"What's your name?"

I didn't care why he was here because I had already figured it out. This kid was an outcast, and he wanted time alone to think— or sing. I could relate. It was probably the reason crawling was such an important part of my identity. Nobody bothered you beneath the surface.

"Shepherd."

"I'm Rayna."

"Thanks for, err…"

The kid was young, so I didn't blame him for his fumbling gratitude. I found it cute in a way that almost made me wish I had a brother. Almost.

"Forget it."

Tears welled in his eyes, and he wiped them away quickly with the sleeve of his now soiled shirt.

"You got it dirty. Your mom is gonna be *pissed*."

He smiled, but only briefly. I crossed my arms over my chest and smiled back.

"I'm cursed." The boy looked at his feet submerged in the inky, black water of the tunnel.

"Aren't we all?"

"Lord Corvus. He doesn't care about us. None of us."

I giggled, and I could see the frown twisting on his face. "I'm not laughing at you."

He waited for an explanation.

"You didn't seriously believe Corvus ever cared about anyone but his own family and their perfect life in the Needle, did you?"

Shepherd shook his head, and I could see the tears of frustration giving way to a steely resolve that ran through the boy in magnetic waves. He might think he was cursed, but I could feel something else in this kid. Power. Strength.

"No. I guess I didn't."

"You keep coming down here for a reason. What is it?" I didn't expect an answer, and that was why the boy's words knocked me back on my heels.

"I can't let it keep happening. I can't. It's not fair."

"Your life looks amazing. Are there seriously problems in the Nest?"

The boy nodded.

"Like what?"

"My family barely has enough to eat. And we're not the only ones. Corvus gives the best stuff to his favorite Crows, and the rest of us have to share what's left."

He was a kid who'd barely left the Nest. I didn't have it my heart to even begin to explain my life as a Crawler. *Former* Crawler. It was no surprise that Corvus ruled in his own best interest. I mean, he didn't even live with the Crows, preferring to hide himself up and away in the Needle.

"So, you come down here and cry about it? You think that's going to change anything?" The comment seemed to draw a new surge of blood to his cheeks, and I could see his mouth tighten. Maybe this kid really was a fighter.

"You wouldn't believe what is happening in the Nest. I might not be an adult like you, but I can do things. And I'm not taking it anymore. It isn't fair."

'Fair' to a kid could mean having to go to bed before the sun completely went down. Thus, I wasn't all that interested in what this Crow had to say next until he spoke again, offering the words that would forever change my life.

"C'mon. I'll show you."

19

The climb up the ladder was only slightly easier than it had been the first time. The boy ascended so quickly that I had to assume he'd been coming down here quite often. And if that was the case, he probably knew more about life in our Hydran village than I had originally thought.

"This way."

Once his body cleared the top, the sunshine nearly blinded me. I had to put my head down and close my eyes as I crawled from the hole in the ground. The birdsong filled my ears, and when I rolled over onto my back in the lush, green grass, I opened my eyes again. The first thing I saw was that perfect, blue sky—the same one I'd seen from my village, and yet somehow different.

"Give me a second." A Crawler asking for a breather would have gotten some serious burn from my friends at the Troll.

I sat up on my elbows and looked around. It looked the same as it had before; a gorgeous interior courtyard lined with plants and flowers like none I'd ever seen. The fountains of stone frogs and fish continued to throw water into the air—rare, precious water. Shepherd was already on the stone pathway leading to the back door of the house, the one I now assumed was his.

Man, this kid really had no clue what "unfair" meant.

"Why me?"

He glanced to the sky before looking into my eyes. "A dream. I saw you there."

Apparently, night visions had the same significance to Crows as they did to Hydrans. My fellow villagers always took note of significant events that we saw in our dreams. The elders claimed that was the place where our subconscious worked through life's mysteries and I had seen this truth in my own life.

"Follow me."

I stood and walked through the flower garden to where Shepherd waited, his hand on the doorknob.

"If they catch you in here, Corvus will execute you."

I shrugged because it would never happen. Maybe it was my foolish confidence or that I somehow knew I had more challenges ahead, but at that moment, I hadn't yet feared for my life. I should have.

"I think I want to see what you need to show me."

"Once we walk through this door and into my house, you'll see everything."

"Okay. Let's go before I change my mind."

Shepherd opened the door, and I followed him inside. I could smell bacon and coffee, and my stomach rumbled. I'd only had bacon once in my life, but I knew what it was as soon as I sniffed the air. Even though it was later in the morning and most of the Hydrans would have put a half-day of work in already, it seemed like the boy's family had still been sleeping. And these were *cursed* Crows.

"I ate all the breakfast, or I would share it with you."

"That's okay," I said, even though it wasn't. Bacon. Damn.

He led me down several hallways, and I could tell just from the feel of the fur beneath my feet that I was in a house within the

Nest. Yes, they had *fur* on the *floor*. Paintings of the Seattle ruins hung on the walls, and I couldn't see a single crack in them. In fact, the surface of the walls looked as smooth as glass, but with the bright sheen of sunflower yellow. None of the chairs had rips in the cushions, and every window had unbroken panes of glass.

Shepherd exited the house out of a side door and snaked through a row of hedges before ducking below a 3-foot wooden fence. I followed.

"Look."

He pointed, and my eyes followed.

A street, but unlike any I'd ever seen in the Hydran village. Only a few people strolled down the main thoroughfare. Yes, Crows definitely kept later work hours. One couple walked and laughed, holding hands. The man wore a woolen coat and pants without wrinkles. The woman wore a white dress, white gloves, and held an object over her head to shield herself from the sun.

The main street's ancient blacktop appeared to be pristine—without weeds, cow dung, or road apples. The buildings lining the street had the same perfect windows as Shepherd's home, and many had flowers growing from boxes attached beneath the sills. I saw one black cat with shiny fur. No wild pigs. No rats.

I guessed Shepherd saw my face because he put his hand on my shoulder and looked into my eyes. "Those aren't Corvax."

"What does it matter?" I wanted to grab the kid by the throat and drag him to my village. Just for the day.

"They get the best clothes, the prime cuts of meat. They get everything, and we don't. It's unfair."

If Shepherd's house was what the cursed Crows had been given, I wasn't sure I really wanted to see how the other Crows lived in the Nest. As if reading my thoughts and feeling the emotions tumbling in my stomach, the kid stood up and walked in the other direction.

"There's more."

Shepherd had turned left at the fence and scampered down

another path. I followed. It snaked down the north side of Queen Anne Hill and, judging from the trees I could see, I knew we were headed to the scrapyard—but from the Nest above, and not from my village below.

Before I could ask, the boy pointed and spoke.

"There."

I couldn't breathe. My knees wobbled, and I almost collapsed to the ground. I wiped at my eyes and let them refocus on the scrapyard one hundred yards away and about twenty feet below us. From this vantage point, I could see the entire yard hidden by the tall fence surrounding it. Near the main gate, the scrap merchant pushed a cart along the fence. He wouldn't be trading until he opened the market in the afternoon.

"This can't be real."

But I knew it was. Piles and piles of aluminum, as far as I could see. The scrap metal that Crawlers had spent years, decades, lifetimes pulling from the depths of the lake and hauling up the hill... it all sat there in the yard. In some places, the piles of metal were so tall that the merchant had clearly had to flatten the tops so that we wouldn't see them from the other side of the fence.

"They don't really need it."

"Huh?"

"The metal," Shepherd said. "They don't need it."

My tongue felt like a hunk of aluminum stuck between two rocks on the bottom of the lake. I kept blinking as if the scrapyard piled high with tons of aluminum was some type of optical illusion. It wasn't.

"Why?"

"My mother says it keeps the Hydran rats fighting over the scraps."

I wanted to punch the kid in the face, but I knew he was only repeating what he'd heard, as most kids did.

"We don't use the metal for much. It just sits there."

He'd answered my next question before I could ask it. I figured I'd have to pick my chin up off the ground if I wanted to talk.

"How long?"

"What do you mean?"

"How long has it been piled there? Like that?" I asked without looking at Shepherd, my eyes unable to turn away from the aluminum tonnage sitting on the hilltop below me.

"Since the beginning."

"Everything I do. Everything we've ever done. All our sacrifices. For *nothing*."

The boy stared at me, but kept his mouth shut.

20

_M_y legs felt like stone as I stumbled toward the village, and my mind drifted as I walked past a group of kids piling sand and mud into pointy castles by the lake. I stopped to watch them for a minute, taking in their faces smeared with dirt, and their shabby, worn clothes hanging life-lessly over bony limbs. Yet, as they played by the lake, their world was free of the strain and torment they had been born into—unburdened by the realization flooding my mind like slow-rising, brackish tidewaters. For now, they would enjoy the flitting igno-rance gifted to them by youth and inexperience. My eyes glazed over as I sighed, their streaking shrills fading into my thoughts.

A cramp gripped my stomach as I turned from the children and stumbled forward, gulping air and grabbing for a thin sapling on the edge of the shore. I stumbled off the lake bank and slipped unseen into long blades of wild grass and clusters of trees near the village outskirts, collapsing at the foot of an old elm while I tried to keep from puking. I'd set off that morning with a stupid curiosity about the Nest, and now I could barely process what I had seen on top of Queen Anne Hill.

I thought back to the couple strolling through the clean

streets in their swanky threads and the smell of bacon. That alone would have been enough to make any Hydran sick. But it was the scrapyard, and the mountains of useless aluminum piled high, that I couldn't stop thinking about. All that crawling... I gasped again as reality set in, and all at once I felt the enormity of my revelation.

Hydrans had been nothing but cogs in the Crows' world. We had been exploited, used, forced to risk our lives gathering metal from the toxic waters for no other reason than to use it to trade for the food *we* grew. My entire life, my grandfather's life—all a sham. Nothing but a system created to keep us occupied while everything good left in this world had been hoarded by the Crows. I had been a Crawler my entire life. My family, my friends, most of my village. We'd done it for years, generations.

"There has to be more to it. They must be saving all of that aluminum for something."

But I knew that wasn't true even as I said it aloud.

"Bullshit. This is total bullshit."

My stomach cramp began to burn, and my heart rattled in my chest. It felt as though my face had caught fire. I couldn't sit there any longer, getting depressed over things that had been set in motion long before I was born. I needed to do something. Tell someone.

But who? Was this really something I wanted to deal with now? It felt too risky, and yet, I knew it wasn't fair.

Grimacing, I remembered how I'd felt when Shepherd had said that to me.

I pushed myself to my feet, slung my bag onto my back, and set off to the village as fast as I could. I needed to tell someone, but not yet. For now, I'd try to put the stockpile of aluminum out of my mind and wait. There would be a time for action later.

As I neared the village square, I noticed crowds of people gathering along the pathways and chatting in hushed tones. They pulled together in huddles and looked into the square with quick, furtive glances. I frowned and pushed my way through the villagers while an eerie silence settled upon us like a dense fog.

The square had been surrounded by armed Crow soldiers—so many that I lost count. For most of us Hydrans, I knew, this was the first time we'd seen Crows since the last insurrection that had taken my parents from me. That cramp in my stomach returned as I looked around, trying to locate Asher or Grandpa, but I couldn't see either of them. At that moment, the crowds on the opposite side of the square parted and my eyes went wide when I saw why.

Pulled by a team of men, the carriage sat upon wooden wheels that bounced over the rough road. As kids, we'd all played in the old Monorail cars, pretending to be Lord Corvus ruling from atop the Needle. Everyone knew he'd had one of the cars restored and converted into his own, private carriage. But from what I could gather from the whispering villagers, he hadn't brought it into the village in decades.

Then another realization hit me, the second in one day to almost knock me over. What if Corvus had found out I'd been inside the Nest? What if he knew that I knew about the aluminum? What if he was here for me?

My vision blurred and I felt dizzy, so that I went stumbling into the man next to me—who gave me a shove upright along with a scowl.

The man driving the carriage pulled his team of Corvax Crows to a halt in the middle of the square. The old rail car stood taller than most of our houses.

"I wonder what brings the crooked vulture from his perch."

I turned to the old woman who'd spoken and gave her a puzzled look instead of an answer. She continued.

"I think Corvus is more rodent than bird if you know what I mean."

The door of the car slid open silently, but it wasn't Lord Corvus who first appeared in the doorway. A servant from inside the car dropped down a set of wooden stairs for the figure who stepped forward next—Aren, the mouthpiece of the Crow leader.

The elderly Crow stood before us then, his sallow face and grave expression matched to the black trench coat flanking his wiry frame.

My stomach churned as the Lord's lapdog stood before our village. He put on a pair of spectacles and unfolded a piece of paper he'd removed from his pocket.

Even the birds fell silent, waiting to hear what he was about to say.

21

*A*fter waiting for about 20 minutes for the rest of the villagers to show up, a flurry of low chattering emerged as Chief Sandor and Aren exchanged a rather cold glance. I noticed the tight curl of the man's thin lips—as though something was permanently wedged up his behind. He continued to sniff at the air and wave his hand in front of his face while his advisors pushed the crowd back, especially shooing away the kids dressed in their filthy rags.

I looked away from Aren to scan the crowd again, this time spotting Silas across the way. He looked back at me, and I gave him a small wave and mouthed the words "Where's Asher?"

He shrugged, frowned, and craned his neck as he looked across the sea of faces. The whole Hydran village had crammed into the square by this time. I knew it would be nearly impossible for Silas to find him, even with his height advantage. I had blown Asher off this morning, hoping he'd understand like he always had. But what if he'd had enough of my stubborn moods?

One of the Crow soldiers cracked a whip, and whatever chatter had started immediately ceased. Aren stood atop the platform with a line of Corvus' soldiers standing on the ground before him. He cleared his throat, although the square had suddenly fallen as silent as a graveyard.

"I am Aren, and I come here today as a representative of Lord Corvus, supreme leader of the Crows, regent of the Lowlands. I am here because of a violation of the most heinous nature."

I shuddered. I wanted to turn and slip from the crowd. I wanted to be anywhere but there. But between the armed Crows patrolling the square and not wanting to leave without Grandpa and Asher, I knew I had to stay.

"Rules and procedures are an important part of our lives. Lord Corvus has entrusted Chief Sandor to uphold these laws and ensure that Hydrans will comply for the betterment of all. These guidelines have been in place for decades; they work for Hydrans, and they work for the Crows so we can co-exist. We each have our roles, which must be honored by every single one of us."

I could feel the blood draining from my face as he continued to read the prepared speech he'd come to deliver on behalf of Lord Corvus.

"One such rule is that under no circumstances should a Hydran ever enter the Nest. Hydrans have been commissioned plots in the Lowlands, and that is your birthright which nobody can take from you."

People nodded and few "hear, hear's" popped up. I bit my tongue, knowing this wasn't where the speech was ending.

"The Crow birthright is the Nest. For generations, we've lived separate but equal existences, each role and boundary clearly defined."

From beneath his brows, his eyes appeared to darken like a thunderstorm on the horizon. He jabbed a long, crooked finger at the villagers. A sudden intake of breath rippled through the people in almost perfect unison. I was pretty sure I felt my rib cage crack from my wild, thumping heart.

Aren gestured at the Chief, who stood silent and stony a few feet away from the make-shift stage. His shoulders slumped as he stared back at Aren, his mouth a straight, tight line.

"It has come to his Lordship's attention that one of you has broken our most sacred vow and entered the Nest."

A collective gasp rose from the crowd, which Aren executed with a single swipe of his arm. He straightened his glasses and looked down again at the speech he'd prepared beforehand.

"This cannot be ignored. When the rules are not honored and obeyed by all, we are left with nothing but anarchy—the kind of chaos that decimated the Old World and left us with what we have today. This level of dishonest insubordination and disrespect cannot be tolerated."

I could feel the villagers turning, their inbred sense of duty to a system they didn't create taking over. The Hydran anger and disgust changed direction like a shifting sea current, moving from being focused on Aren to suspecting their fellow villagers in the square.

"But Lord Corvus is a fair and benevolent ruler. Nobody in this village has starved to death. Nobody has ever been wrongly imprisoned."

He paused, and I saw heads nodding in agreement.

"Therefore, he is willing to show mercy to the individual and also not punish the entire village for the transgression of one. If the person responsible comes forward, I can assure you that no harm will come to you, but you must confess your misconduct at once."

This couldn't be happening. I was dreaming again, right? Did Aren know it was me, or was he bluffing, unsure if any Hydran had been in the Nest?

Nobody made a sound as Aren lowered his note and scanned the village. When his eyes locked on mine, I wanted the ground to swallow me.

"Can you imagine life without the metal merchant and the ration trade? You'd have no access to our fields, and you'd be forced to scour the ruins or the untamed forests for food. Have you seen what creatures lurk in those dark recesses? I have it on good authority that some settlements don't even have access to water, and that they wage war for control of life's most basic necessities. One place, Erehwon, is rumored to murder infants."

He waited, allowing the fearful description of the remote parts of a world left behind to fill our imaginations. Parents told stories of the wild places closer to home to keep children from wandering too far from the village. Leaving the Lowlands came with dire consequences.

"Think about that and the protection we afford this village. Because if this transgression is not accounted for, our Lord may be forced to sever the official document binding our societies together."

Sandor looked around, his eyes boring holes through a group of young Crawlers. Had Sandor told Aren about our talk? Although the Chief had been disappointed in me, we were both Hydrans and I surmised that he might protect me from the wrath of Corvus for as long as he could, simply out of that shared loyalty.

"Nothing? Nobody?"

A new energy had pulsed through the crowd. Some of the elders had said that Aren had ice water running through his veins, that he could appear calm and unshaken and yet hide a tornado inside. And I was about to witness that firsthand.

"Very well. In order not to damage our relationship or threaten the system we've lived within for generations, I will designate the punishment on behalf of the hidden offender, and then we will all move on with our day."

The sigh from the villagers had been filled with relief—but it was proven to be a short respite as Aren continued.

"That one," he said to the closest guard while pointing at a boy who couldn't have been more than seven years old. "He will do."

The boy's parents put their arms around him, but two more

soldiers joined the first one, ripping the child away in a flurry of tears. Sandor stepped forward, but Aren glared at him, and finally the village leader took a step back.

"If the guilty party will not pay for his disobedience, then this boy will. We need a sacrificial lamb or the entire system crumbles. I promise the offender that you will not be executed. But if you hide like a coward, this unfortunate, unavoidable, action will be on you."

I swallowed hard but couldn't dislodge the hunk of guilt caught in my throat. Time felt as though it had begun to move faster.

Aren pointed to the boy as he spoke, and I knew what was about to happen as the events unfolded before me.

"Last chance."

When nobody spoke, Aren did. "Off with the boy's head."

The kid squealed out as one of the Crow soldiers gripped his elbow and pulled him forward. His mother screamed as his father held her back.

The father called out then. "Whoever it was, speak up. Damn you!"

I didn't know what to do. If I confessed, who would take care of my grandfather. But I couldn't stand by and watch Aren execute an innocent kid. I started to raise my hand, but I was too late.

"It was me!"

The voice had shot through the square and seemed to ring in my ears like a phantom bell. I swallowed hard, and my heart sank as I saw Asher pushing his way through the crowd and stepping in front of the platform. He lifted his head, his chin up and his eyes locked on Aren.

"I entered the Nest. It was me."

I couldn't believe what I'd heard.

Aren regarded Asher with a long, precise stare before motioning the soldier to release the boy.

"Apprehend him. Justice will be restored in the Lowlands, and his Lordship will be pleased."

Two soldiers sidled up next to Asher and grabbed him by the wrists.

My head whirled. I couldn't let it go down like this—I had to do something. I took a deep breath and raised my arms high.

I stepped forward, and called out as loudly as I could. "No! It wasn't Asher. It was me! I went into the Nest."

After a wave of grumbling moved through the crowd, Aren turned his head sideways and looked at me. "Excuse me?"

I pushed my way through the villagers until I was ten feet from the stage. "It wasn't him."

Asher looked at me, his eyes pleading for me to shut up. He knew me well enough to know I wouldn't; when I thought about it later, I'd understand that what he claimed next wasn't surprising.

"That Crawler is a liar. Always telling stories to make herself look better than the rest."

I heard Jaef's snicker above the crowd's whisperings. It wasn't true, and Asher knew it. I never lied about my hauls. Ever.

"I went through the tunnel. Saw the fountains, the house, the flower gardens. It was me. I entered the Nest."

Aren nodded, and the soldiers bound Asher's wrists together. I looked at Sandor, but he had been staring down at his feet. The villagers chirped, some shouting while others clapped.

My heart sank as Asher turned away from me to accept his fate.

22

I lost sight of Asher as the soldiers hustled him to the rickety stage. The crowd thrummed as they surged forward, some to hurl insults at me while others waved accusatory fingers at Asher. Within moments, the village's subdued uncertainty grew into riotous shouting. Using my shoulders to push through the crowd, I tried to keep my eyes on Asher.

Aren's voice cut through the commotion. "Hush, hush!"

The shouts dwindled to whispers, villagers' eyes shifting between Aren and the soldiers who had dragged the man in front of him. I'd made some headway and now stood at the foot of the stage where I could see Asher perfectly. I wanted to scream at him, but he gazed into the dirt, his head down. He was purposely avoiding me. I just knew it.

One of Corvus' advisors appeared with a piece of paper and quill in hand. The elderly man scurried through the square in his long white robes, coming to a stop next to Asher, who didn't even flinch at the man's arrival.

Aren shifted his stare to Asher.

"You have confessed to breaking a binding agreement

between our societies and have illegally entered the Nest. I did promise the person responsible would be spared from execution, should they come forth... and here you stand, bound and shamed before your people. The people you've betrayed."

A few hunks of rotten squash landed at Asher's feet along with several insults thrown from the people pressing against the front of the stage. Still, his eyes never left the ground, even when I noticed his lips pinched together.

Damn you, Asher. Why couldn't you just have kept your mouth shut?

"The guilty party shall read and sign this confession."

Aren slammed the paper down on a table dragged onto the stage by one of the guards. The Crow leader must have had this document written already, knowing whoever did it would confess under pressure.

"Confession will spare your life, son."

Aren had thrust a quill into Asher's hand as he'd whispered those words to my friend.

Asher slowly raised his eyes and looked blankly at the document before giving a slight nod.

The crowd let loose with another barrage of curses and protests. I couldn't tell if their fury was directed at Aren or Asher. The longer this spectacle wore on, the more worried I became. Sandor and Aren had done it this way for a reason. I couldn't figure out why the confessional wasn't taking place in Sandor's house, like most other village negotiations.

I would understand soon enough.

The guards moved, and unbound Asher's wrists, and as he grasped the quill from Aren in his right hand, the entire village became so quiet that I could hear the inky tip scratching the paper as he scrawled his name. The old man in the robes snatched the document from Asher as soon as he was done. My friend gazed up at Aren for the first time since his confession.

Aren's eyes bore into Asher's, the man's thin lips curved ever so slightly as he turned to face the rest of the villagers. My fingers knotted and twisted as I noticed Asher's jaw clench. He must have felt it, too. A feeling that whatever Corvus had planned, and had sent Aren to implement, hadn't been finished yet. Time slowed, and the silence weighed heavy on us all. A few children coughed, filling the awkward void with any kind of noise they could muster. I felt a tightness in my stomach, sweat breaking on the back of my neck. Aren wasn't done with Asher.

And right before it happened, I understood what Aren was doing. He wasn't just punishing Asher... he was punishing *all* of us. He would make sure that no Hydran ever attempted even a glance at the Nest ever again.

With a fast flick of his wrist, Aren waved the handkerchief at his guards. They rushed to his side, and again I had the feeling that this entire procedure had been rehearsed and entirely expected.

"Because you have confessed, you will be spared execution."

I held my breath. For a split second, I thought I might have been wrong.

"But, according to the confessional agreement you read and signed, you will be forever marked for your transgression, as a reminder and a warning to your fellow Hydrans that the laws of the Lowlands are supreme, greater than any Chief or Lord." Aren shot a look at Sandor before continuing. "Without order, there is anarchy. And in anarchy, there lies only death."

A woman gasped.

"Off with his right hand."

Now, events moved so quickly that I felt as if my brain couldn't process what my eyes saw. The guard on Asher's left drew his sword while the other pinned my friend's arm to the table, the soldier holding Asher by the elbow and hand. Aren crossed his arms over his chest while the old man in the robes stepped back. Groans and cries came from the crowd, none of which could drown out the wall of sound in my head. I felt as though I was deep beneath the lake where sounds were distorted into nothing but auditory hauntings.

Asher's piercing scream cut through my head as the soldier's blade cut through my friend's wrist, the quill still squashed beneath his fingers. Blood sprayed the old man's robes, and Aren used his handkerchief to wipe a drop of Asher's blood from his cheek.

Once Asher collapsed to his knees, the guards dragged him away toward the healer's hut while Aren looked at Sandor once more before making his final statements to the villagers.

"I trust that order shall be kept within the village and that we shall have no further infractions, or Lord Corvus will be forced to take more serious measures."

Whatever rebellious energy had sparked the crowd earlier had been bled like Asher. Nobody spoke. Nobody moved. The kids who had been coughing didn't make a sound.

"Crawlers may continue to bring their hauls to the gate of the scrapyard. The metal merchant will set the day's exchange rate, as always. But, know this. No Hydran is permitted in or near the Nest. Ever. His Lordship will not be so gracious or understanding, should it happen again."

*a*ren remained.

I thought for sure he'd immediately be whisked back into his Corvax-drawn carriage and driven down to the fortified base of the Needle to report the events to Lord Corvus. And I wanted to run after Asher and help, but my feet wouldn't move. Would he ever want to see me again?

The coppery, bitter smell of blood filled the air as some of the villagers trudged back to the lake or the fields, but most stayed. Sandor and Aren hadn't parted ways, and it looked as if they'd had a heated exchange at a level that only they could hear.

Sandor dropped his head to his chest, and Aren lifted his chin high to address the crowd once more.

My eyes fell on the trail of blood smearing the ground. I began to feel sick a moment later when I saw Asher's blood and his severed hand lying on the old table—the hand I'd held in my own on warm, summer nights. I tore my eyes away, unable to stop the bile rising in my throat. I doubled over and gagged, determined not to be sick and give Aren and his goons the satisfaction.

Aren walked to the edge of the stage where Jaef and several of our best Crawlers had gathered to watch the spectacle. The Crow leader's mouthpiece addressed them, but with a volume and intensity in his voice that suggested he wanted others to hear it, as well—including Sandor. I looked at our Chief, but he stood gazing into the distance toward the great sea, his skin as pale as goat's milk.

"For the next month, the village's daily aluminum hauls have been doubled. If you fail to deliver, then I will return. And, next time, Lord Corvus won't just be taking the hand of some nosey, lowly farmer."

I groaned. Sandor and Aren looked at me at the same time, as both were close enough to hear it. I thought I might vomit. I had been disgusted by the violence used on my friend. And, at that moment, I hadn't been sure why I'd done what I had.

"Does she take issue?" Aren asked Sandor, clearly knowing that I could hear and answer on my own.

"I don't feel well," I said.

"Shut. Her. Up. *Chief.*"

Sandor grimaced and then took a step toward me. "Speaking now is completely inappropriate, Rayna."

I nodded, and Aren smiled.

"Bring the carriage," he said to the soldiers. "I believe we've restored order in amongst these disobedient primitives. Wouldn't you agree, Chief Sandor?"

Sandor said nothing, his lips pursed in a grim line as he conceded with a nod. His dark eyes briefly glanced my way as Aren about-turned and marched back to Corvus' monorail wagon with his men in tow.

$\mathcal{M}$y legs felt like pudding as I wandered down the village street and headed to the healer's hut. People swarmed around the filthy canvas held up with old hemp rope and twisted tree branches. They chatted quietly near the closed flap, their faces white as Asher's moans filled the air. As I drew closer, I clutched at the end of my braid, as if holding my hair would stabilize my shaky legs. It didn't help.

When I approached, they all stopped talking, and one man held up his right hand and put it in my face. "The boy is undergoing emergency treatment. Stay back."

I didn't recognize the man, but several others looked at me, and it became clear that everyone had been both horrified by what they thought had been Asher's foolish behavior and, at the same time, disgusted by Sandor's inability to protect us from the Crow leader's punishments. If a Chief couldn't protect his people, what was the point?

Another one of Asher's muted groans floated into my ears, and I gasped, my eyes darting desperately to the canvas flap.

"He's my friend. I want to see Asher."

"The healer is tending to his... wound. Come back tomorrow."

My cheeks burned, which I knew would not look unusual—or guilty—given the circumstances. "I just want to see if he's okay."

"Well, Aren took his hand while our Chief watched!" the man snapped while the others all nodded and murmured in agreement. "Do you *think* Asher is 'okay?'"

I took a step back and almost stumbled on the gravel. Asher let loose with another long grunt, the painful sound tearing at my heart.

"Didn't you hear me, girl? Come back tomorrow!"

I nodded, and had already turned around when I heard my name.

"Rayna!"

Asher's mother stumbled from the hut, racing toward me. The man huffed and shook his head, turning his back on us both to rejoin the other whispering villagers, uncertain whether the blame for this tragedy should be placed on Asher, Sandor, Aren, or Corvus. Or possibly all four.

My lips trembled as she caught me in a hug and I buried my face in her chest while trying to fight back the tears. I had always been close to Asher's mother, Ember. She had been the only adult female I'd really had in my life, and she'd always treated me so kindly. Today was no exception.

"Oh, Ember. I'm so sorry. How is he?"

She held me at arm's length and mustered a weak smile. Her watery, blue eyes were dim and bloodshot over sullen dark circles. She shook her grey-streaked head.

"It's not your fault, honey. He'll get through... he's a fighter. I'll make sure he knows you're thinking of him. I have to get back inside."

I wouldn't have known myself, but I'd heard mothers saw their children differently than others did. Asher was sweet, sensitive, kind, and strong. But a fighter? I hadn't really seen that side of him.

"Okay," I said, my words barely a whisper. "I'll come back tomorrow."

As I watched her race back to her son, it took everything I had not to collapse to the ground. I turned away and swallowed the lump in my throat. It *was* my fault. It should have been me in that hut with a bleeding stump for a hand, not Asher.

I ran from the healer's hut with guilt burning inside of me, suffocating, constricting.

*T*he air was still and the wind chimes silent when I stepped from behind one of the Chief's advisors and into the house. The door slammed behind me, and I shot a wide-eyed look around the room. They certainly had a thing for door-slamming around here. I shook my head as I turned around. The distinct odor of broccoli and onion chowder clung to the walls, and a half-empty bowl sat near the candle burning in the center of the table. Sandor leaned in with his elbows on the table and his hands folded under his chin, watching me.

"Doors bother you, Rayna?"

"Not usually."

"But closed doors? They bother you, don't they?"

I bit my lip. I hadn't come here to discuss doors.

"No."

He sat back in his chair and looked at me, his eyes never leaving mine.

"I don't believe you. I think your curiosity drives you mad, not knowing what is under lock and key. You like to open doors, am I right?"

I shrugged. "Some doors are better opened."

"And some doors are better left shut," he said, the deep timbre of his words reverberating off the walls.

I shuddered, my eyes dropping to the single flame on the table. I knew we weren't really talking about doors. I guessed he already knew why I was here, although I wasn't so sure. I had come to Sandor seeking atonement, or maybe hoping to unload my guilt on someone else so I wouldn't be reminded of it every time I looked at Asher.

"I have a wild notion why you're here today. So, why don't you just go ahead and say it?"

I blinked, licked my lips, and steeled myself. "I was the one in the Nest, not Asher."

He was silent for a moment as his dark eyes crawled over me. For the first time, I had explicitly confessed, leaving no ambiguity between us.

"Like I said, doors."

"Yes." I looked away again.

"And now you see the consequences of your actions, and what it means for Hydrans. For Asher. Now you see what happens when we break the rules."

"I do. I'm sorry. I should have—"

"Sorry won't restore your friend's hand, nor scavenge the impossible aluminum haul imposed upon our village, will it?" His words rattled the windows in the house.

I shook my head and swallowed my tears along with my pride. The dishonor I'd brought upon my grandfather had formed as a cramp in my stomach. For a moment, I thought it'd be less painful to have my hand cut off than to face the disappointment on Grandpa's face when he heard the truth about what had happened in the village square that day.

"For now, your guilt is your punishment. Perhaps another transgression would call for a stiffer penalty, but not now. You will serve this village differently."

I cocked my head to the side and looked at Sandor. He was no longer lecturing me, but instead talking to me more like an adult than he ever had before.

"I need you to crawl again, starting tomorrow."

My eyes flew open, my jaw agape as I looked at him.

"Huh?"

"The increased hauls demanded by Corvus are practically impossible...without a talented Crawler. I know you're the best. The other Crawlers tell me as much."

For a split second, I was wondering who he'd spoken to about my hauls—who would have told him the truth, that is.

Warring thoughts battled in my head. I had loved crawling and it was the thing I was made to do. And if I started again on Sandor's orders, it would keep Corvus off our backs. But then in my head I saw the heaps of aluminum on Queen Anne Hill and I almost told the Chief about it. I decided against telling him of the lie we'd all been living. At that time, it still felt too dangerous and I honestly wasn't sure what to do.

"Whatever I can do to help the village." I turned away with a grimace on my face. For now, I would crawl again and figure the rest out later.

"Rayna."

I turned my head to face Sandor, one hand on the door while looking over my shoulder.

"Tomorrow, report to Jaef. He will be supervising your crawls."

I started to laugh.

"Are you serious? That jerk can't get enough decent hauls on his own, let alone while supervising me—or anyone else for that matter. He's incompetent, he's a thief, and I don't trust him."

Sandor leaned back in his chair and folded his hands together on the table. His nostrils flared, and his eyes tightened.

"You'd rather face Corvus? Explain to him that not only were you the one to disobey the laws of the Lowlands, but that you stood by and let your friend accept your punishment?"

I sighed and clenched my teeth together. "No, sir."

"Then we have an understanding?"

"Yes, sir."

"Good," he said, ushering me out the door with a flick of his hand.

I took my time walking home. I kicked at rocks and trash as I mulled over the new turn of events. When I approached Asher's home, I stopped and stared at the old timber door. The hut sat in silence, yet I knew he was probably in there by now, sleeping off the herbal painkillers the healer would've given him.

The villagers had not followed Asher or his mother to their house. It almost seemed as if Asher had been tainted, the immediate pity from the villagers having evaporated into a quiet condemnation.

I wanted to see him and tell him I was sorry, to let him know I cared. But the toxic twist of guilt roped through me mercilessly. I whirled my head around, unable to look at his house a moment longer. I quickened my pace and ran the rest of the way home.

2 6

J wanted to hit him. No. More than that. I wanted to watch the teeth fly from his mouth as I knocked them out one punch at a time. It had only been a few days, and already the sound of Jaef's voice sent a shiver down my spine—and it wasn't the feel-good variety, either. I stared at his flapping lips as he spoke useless words, bossing me around. He took great pleasure in filling his new role as my supervisor, and I took greater pleasure in imagining all the ways I could hurt him. Of course, I knew I had to suck it up. At least I was crawling again, and staying busy helped to keep my mind off Asher. I still hadn't seen him since the incident. I still hadn't decided who I would tell about the aluminum heaps behind the walls guarded by the metal merchants. Although that secret would need to be exposed, it also felt dangerous—like swimming out into the unknown currents of the great Pacific.

"Rayna, hello? Are you listening?"

I glanced up at Jaef as he pointed toward a steep-sided bank of black mud submerged in the water.

"You can't be serious? There's nothing over there."

He grimaced while winking at his friends who stood along the shore, snickering.

"How would you know that if you haven't dived there yet?"

"Because I'm not an idiot," I said, gesturing toward the obvious coal pit. I knew it. And so did he. "There's no metal at the bottom of that pit. Just coal."

My lips curled, and I turned away from him to drop my diving gear on the dirty sand. We'd been crawling for a few hours, and I needed to take a break and give my lungs a rest before going back in the water.

Jaef walked up behind me and grabbed my arm. I whirled around to face him with a glare and an insane itch to scratch out his beady, green eyes.

"All I ever hear is *Rayna* this, *Rayna* that. *Rayna*, the best Crawler in the village." He edged his nose closer until it almost touched mine. "Impress me. Pull something from the pit."

His breath stunk like garlic and cabbage. I snatched my arm from his grip and stepped back while trying not to gag.

"Get your hands off me. I'm not going near that pit."

A chorus of oooh's rose from behind us.

Jaef's face reddened as he grabbed my arm again. "Fine. I think Sandor will be interested to know you're not following orders. You know what'll happen now, don't ya?"

He glanced at his friends, who had come up behind him. "Someone want to remind this princess?"

The tallest goon smirked. "Yeah, she'll be banished into the woods and become dinner for the wild night creatures."

"Nah, that's too easy for her," another guy said, ribbing his friend with an elbow before looking straight at me. "She'll be sent away to one of those prison cities."

There was a rumble of laughter at my expense. I could feel my face burning, and I dug the nails on my curved fingers into my palm. One punch to the face. That's all I wanted.

"Then she'll really have to crawl—on her knees, begging for

mercy for the rest of her miserable life," Jaef said, looking at me with a wide smirk. "Is that what you want, *princess?*"

He emphasized the S and my stomach knotted like it was full of sour milk. I turned my back on them and squeezed my eyes shut while slowly counting to five.

One.

Damn Jaef.

Two.

Breathe, Rayna, breathe.

Three.

Damn Lord Corvus to hell.

Four.

And Chief Sandor for making me crawl under Jaef.

Five.

Double damn Asher and his stupid loyalty and his bravery, too.

Well, that didn't work. Grandpa had always told me that counting to five would temper my anger, but I felt sure he'd never had to deal with this creep. I stamped my foot into the rocky turf. My jaw jutted with the clench of my teeth as I saddled my hands on my hips and glowered.

"I suppose you would need a girl to do your dirty work, Jaef. It's clear you lack in certain manly attributes." I lowered my gaze to his crotch.

His smug expression fell from his face as his friends burst into laughter. He spit on the ground in front of his buddies, so that their laughter stifled, but they paid attention to how he would respond to my insult of his manhood.

Jaef grabbed his crotch with his right hand while thrusting his narrow hips forward. "If you *were* under me, you wouldn't have any complaints in that department." He paused and moved his eyes over my breasts. "But I wouldn't touch you with Silas' dick. So, I suggest you get back to work while *we* take a break, because you can't touch this."

More crotch thrusting. A break? I wanted to show him what a

break felt like between his legs. I scuffed my foot across the ground in that general direction as I swiveled on my heels and grabbed my gear. He nodded slightly, and I grunted as I picked up my bag and adjusted my Bright.

I'd out-haul all of them combined. At least I'd walk away with that sliver of satisfaction.

27

---

y hair was clumped together with a thick layer of black mud. I reeked. I knew it, and so did everyone else who happened to come within a few feet of me as we dropped off our hauls at the scrapyard later that afternoon. Naturally, Jaef found my stench rather amusing and milked it for all he could, wafting his hand in front of his nose and pointing at me for all to see.

I'd tried wiping the mud from my face, but it had only smeared across my skin. I'd given up trying to be presentable and instead pulled the cart along in the line. Not only did mud stink, but the oily mixture of coal residue and lake algae was almost impossible to clean off. The metal merchants continued bellowing the usual commands, moving the trading along with their gnarled hands and crooked, craven smirks. I ignored the stares and snickers being cast my way and kept my eyes on the Crawler in front of me.

"That's right, folks. It's her." Jaef pointed a finger at me. "She wanted to play in the black mud, and I couldn't refuse. Like attracts like, I say. Right, Rayna? Feeling like royalty yet?"

I turned, dropped the handle of my cart. "I pulled a few cans from that black mud. More than the rest of your crew did the entire day."

That was true. There was no way I'd been about to crawl through that coal pit and come up to the surface empty-handed.

"Your cans are probably worth nothing with that filth on them."

"We'll see what the metal merchant has to say about my haul."

"Oh? I'm glad you're so confident in your metal because you're going right back in the mud first thing tomorrow."

My teeth ground together as I bit down to keep profanities from shooting from my mouth.

"You can't be serious? It's not crawling–it's a pig bath."

His nose flared, and he leaned closer to me as he made a big show of sniffing the air. "You certainly smell like a pig–oink."

The others laughed as Jaef gave me a deliberate wink before high-fiving his friends.

I closed my eyes, feeling the blood rushing through my veins like molten lava. I wasn't sure how long I could tolerate it. All of it.

"Did you get dropped on the head as a child? Is that why you're such an ass?"

He flashed a grin at me. "Why don't you just leave, pig? You're polluting the air. We'll take it from here."

Without another word, I shoved the cart handle at him and stalked away while his friends oinked at me. I was so angry that I left my cart and my place in line for the ration exchange, the very thing I needed to keep my grandfather alive. My blood boiled, and my head itched from the mud cementing my scalp. It would take me an hour to rinse it off and then I'd be back in there tomorrow. Not to mention putting up with Jaef's insults the entire time.

"To hell with this."

I charged down the hill toward the village's biggest house. I saw nothing and everything at the same time, my mind in turmoil with injustice, ridicule, and fury. I marched through the village, avoiding the dismal expressions of the Hydrans scraping by with only the bare essentials while Corvus and the Crows lived on us, literally and figuratively.

The heels of my boots smacked the floorboards of Sandor's porch, and the guards standing out front did nothing. That is until they got in my face.

Dickhead Number One blocked the door. "Chief Sandor isn't accepting guests." He looked from my mud-caked head to my filthy boots. "Nor beggars."

"You know who I am, and I demand to see the Chief at once."

Dickhead Number Two towered over me. "Turn around. Go home."

I nodded and took two steps toward the front walk before turning around and barreling back at the door, my fists pounding on the weather-worn pine. The door flew open, and I almost punched Sandor in the nose with the meat of my fist.

His black eyes stared at me, his lips tightly pursed. He gestured for me to follow him with a flick of his head before disappearing into the house again. I couldn't help but smirk at the guards as I crossed the threshold.

I entered the darkened room, blinking as my eyes adjusted from the daylight outside. It took a few moments before I saw Sandor standing on the far side of the room. The dimmest side of the room. The two guards had stormed in after me, but Sandor raised his hand for them to stop, and nodded. They exhaled as they walked back outside.

"Why am I not surprised you're here?"

I didn't know what to make of his comment. Was my behavior that predictable?

"I can't do this anymore. Jaef is forcing me to crawl places where he knows there isn't any metal. He's doing it just to be an asshole."

"That *asshole* is your direct superior. He will tell you when and where to crawl. I thought I'd made that clear to you." The Chief shook his head as he walked over to his table and sat down. "Did you gather a haul from your assigned dive?"

"Yes, but that's not the point. I'm better than all of them combined. I know where to crawl and how to get the most off the bottom of the lake. He's wasting my time, but more importantly, he's wasting your time. And the village's resources. He's putting his own dislike for me in front of the needs of the village. How are we supposed to meet the increased demands when Jaef is sending me into coal pits?"

His chest inflated, and his broad shoulders heaved as his eyes burned into mine.

"You seem to have misunderstood the terms of your punishment. You have violated our laws and brought suffering to our people. Have you seen Asher's wound yet? I don't care how fair or unfair Jaef is treating you. Trust me when I say that Corvus would do much worse."

I recoiled and stepped back from him, my downturned eyes locked on the tops of my muddy boots.

"Tomorrow, you will report to Jaef, and he will assign your crawls. Is that clear?"

I nodded.

"I said, *is that clear?*"

I looked up and into Sandor's eyes, my tears gathering and held back only by my stubborn pride. "Yes, *sir*."

28

Guilt is a funny thing. If I could give it a color, I think I'd shade it green. Not the bright luminous green of rolling hills, but the murky brown-sludgy green I'd sift through at the bottom of the lake. Green was also the color of the bland broccoli soup I had just finished serving up for dinner.

I wandered into the living room and handed Grandpa his bowl. "Eat up. Broccoli is good for you."

His white beard brushed across his shoulder as he looked up at me. My heart lurched. More and more, he reminded me of a little boy.

"Thank you, hon." His voice trembled with a soft hum.

His spotted fingers shook as he reached for the bowl, his watery eyes struggling to focus as he brought the spoon to his mouth.

"Careful, it's hot." I sat in a chair next to him.

"I know. I'm not a child."

Sometimes I thought he could read my mind. I looked down at my own bowl and pushed my spoon through the green broth. I hated broccoli soup, and I had already binged on guilt.

Grandpa slurped some broth before setting down his spoon

and looking at me.

"Okay. What's wrong? Your face is as green as this soup."

Sometimes all it took to lose control was someone you loved expressing their concern. The tears rolled silently down my cheeks, and before I knew it, I could barely breathe.

Grandpa's bony hands offered me a torn handkerchief, and for just a moment, I allowed myself to really feel the torrent of emotions ripping through me. My body shook as I leaned against his frail frame. When I'd been a child, he'd always been my safe place, and as much as I wanted to be the caregiver now, I understood that he would always be my grandpa.

"It can't be that bad. Life is ever-changing, remember... it will pass."

I pulled back and gazed at him through my tears.

"It *is* that bad. Asher's hand was cut off because of me—because I disobeyed and went into the Nest. He is innocent, and now he has no hand."

His faded blue eyes looked at me without judgment or condemnation. All I saw was love and tenderness which I thought might break me down even more.

He shook his head. "Rayna, Rayna. Please listen to me. I know I've said it before—guilt is a wasted emotion. You cannot rise above guilt, and you cannot live with it. Whatever happens in life, let it happen and know that there is always a higher purpose. An unseen plan for all of us. You didn't cut off your friend's hand, did you?"

"No, but it was because of me. He took the blame—I should have tried to—"

"Tried what? Offered them your hand instead?"

"Yes!"

"Asher made a choice. He protected you, gave himself up to spare you. Have you thought about that? He made choices, too."

My brows furrowed. This wasn't the conversation I'd anticipated. It *was* my fault.

"But he's innocent."

"Not anymore. He lied to Sandor. Aren. And, therefore, to Corvus." He leaned back in his chair and waited for me to consider an angle I hadn't been able to see while buried by my own selfish feelings.

Asher disobeyed and had been punished for it. It had been his choice to lie.

"The situation is out of your control. What has been done is done. Guilt will not serve you here, nor in any situation in life."

I looked back at him silently. He appeared pale and drawn, the skin around his eyes sunken as his focus began to fade out again. I knew I'd just lost him to another world somewhere deep inside of his own deteriorating brain. I rose to my feet and leaned in to kiss his forehead. He felt cold under his blanket.

"I'll fetch you more socks." I darted from the room to get the only other pair he owned.

"Are you going to finish your soup?" he asked as I pulled the ripped socks over his feet.

I forced a smile. No way could I stomach food. I needed to think, to walk and figure out the thoughts churning in my head.

"No, you can have it. I'll be back in a bit, okay?"

He nodded and mumbled something else about regrets and that the air would do me well before slurping the now cold soup from my bowl. The coherent stretches between his wandering attention spans seemed to be shrinking.

I pulled on my boots, stood up, and looked at him again. The old man before me did remind me of a child, not the grandfather who had just comforted me with his wise advice. As I pulled the door shut behind me, I decided that I would make him more magic tea when I returned.

The tip of my nose stung in the cool night air as I walked through empty village streets and alleyways. Wild cats rummaged through the trash and fought with each other for the scraps, their cries filling the darkness like tortured souls.

I walked to the lake and sat along the shore where the still water gleamed, an iridescent trail to the full moon staring down with a cold brilliance. I hadn't often seen the lake at night, and as I fixed my eyes on the tranquil water, I was captivated by its simple beauty. I wished with all my heart I could surrender my secrets, my thoughts, and my guilt to the lake that shone under the moon.

I sat there for the longest time and mulled over everything that had happened. I knew the unsettling feeling inside of me needed to be resolved. I had to come to peace with the raging guilt, as Grandpa advised. I needed to stop blaming myself and find peace with everything that had happened, and accept everything that would, including Jaef and his utter stupidity. And maybe it was time I told Grandpa about the piles of aluminum I'd seen?

And I needed Asher. I missed my friend.

I thought that if I stayed there long enough, perhaps the moon would snatch away my inner turmoil and give me the certainty I longed for. As it was, my bones began to freeze under my thin jacket and a sudden urge to pee overwhelmed me. I retraced my steps back home at a much quicker pace than my trek there, stopping short when I saw Asher's mother, Ember, standing in front of my hut.

She rushed toward me, clasping my hands when she reached my side.

"Rayna. I've been looking everywhere for you. Asher wants to see you. Come."

"Really?"

She smiled and tugged at my hands. "Yes."

As we walked toward their hut, I couldn't help but take one last look at the moon. She seemed to be smiling down at me now. Maybe the moon had been listening to my thoughts. Maybe the moon would make this all go away.

29

The curtains were tainted with age-old stains and patches of white from over-scrubbing and too much sun. Their shabby ends dangled lifelessly from the broken windows. They were there for the same reason as the chipped, faded frames with the flaked images on the walls—all of it signaled Ember's attempts at making their disintegrating hut a home. But the effort was ineffective and made in vain, and only served as a reminder of all that once was.

And all that would never be.

I had always hated those frames that hung crooked along the walls in Asher's hut. They had always depressed me. Ember used to say they were her inspiration. She'd often tell us that, if we could imagine it, we could create it. Well, I'd spent more time than I'd cared to admit on imagination. Yet, still, I remained here. My inspiration couldn't be framed like those ripped, aging images.

Asher was sitting by the fire when I walked into the hut, his eyes closed within his pale face and his breathing raspy. I approached and sat next to him without saying a word.

He must have sensed me because his eyes fluttered open, his

lips instantly curving into a smile. When he gazed at me, I thought my heart would break.

"Hi," I said, dropping my eyes to his lap and his bandaged arm. I wasn't sure what to expect. Did he hate me?

"Hi."

I gulped back the lump in my throat and leveled my gaze at him. He had to hate me.

"Are you about to tell me that you never want to see me again?"

I couldn't help it. I'd had to get straight to the point.

He grimaced and shook his head. I held my breath and braced myself for whatever he was about to say.

"Seriously, Rayna? It's not always about you. You know that, right?"

"Since when?"

"Since I lost my hand for you."

I shut my mouth. What could I say to that?

He lifted his bandaged wrist and flinched before easing it back into his lap.

"You owe me one."

My eyes filled with tears. I felt my chest begin to tremble and my vision blurred.

"Oh, Asher. I'm so sorry. What have I done?"

He said nothing and just watched me for a second, his eyes glimmering under the glowing flames as he shook his head.

"Hey, at least they didn't cut out my tongue."

I'm not sure I could ever have faced my friend again if Aren had done anything more to him.

"I'm sorry for not listening to you. I should have. I'm an idiot. I promise I'll always listen to you from now on."

"No, you won't. That's what I've always liked about you." He smiled. "You never do what you're told. You do what's right."

Why was he so good to me? I wanted him to hate me so it would be easier to go back to my awful, new life as Jaef's underling. I searched Asher's face for any trace of bitterness. I found nothing but affection.

"Asher?"

"Yeah?"

"Can I hug you?"

"You don't need to ask," he said, lifting his good arm so I could lean against him.

I listened to him breathe as I gazed at the fire. I felt as if the flames were twisting and burning inside of me. How would I make this right? Could I make this right?

His lips brushed across my hair and I looked up at him, his eyes drooping and his head bobbing to one side.

"Rayna?"

"Yeah?"

He closed his eyes, and I heard the faintest of whispers pass his lips before he fell asleep.

"You're all I ever wanted."

30

The mud oozed between my fingers. Even with the beam of my Bright, I could barely see a thing through the brown water as I probed and combed along the edges of the mud pit. I tried to keep the vile grit from getting in my nose, but it was nearly impossible.

A flash of silver caught my eye. I hesitated. I knew I'd need to dislodge a whole new bloom of dirt to extricate the metal, and I couldn't be sure it was even aluminum until I could get some of it uncovered to check it against my Band. I looked at the scrap metal and thought about Jaef making me crawl down here again. It was bullshit, but I didn't have many choices right now.

It was a can, and as I pulled it from the muck, I inwardly cursed Jaef.

By the time my lungs emptied of air, I'd scored enough loot from the sludge to hopefully satisfy Jaef's need to belittle me more that day. Well, I could hope, right?

As I broke the surface of the water, I spotted him and his stupid friends sitting along the shoreline taking their break. They were nibbling on carrots and stale bread while horsing around in their usual way. I climbed from the water and approached, a few of them breaking out into pig grunts as I did. I ignored them and swung my full bag from my back, dropping it at Jaef's feet.

"Is that all you got?"

My heart sank. *Here we go again.*

"Well, it's not the easiest place to crawl. I think I got some cans that were there a long time..." My voice trailed off, waiting for his reply.

His long, nimble fingers reached for the bag and fondled the drawstring.

"Hmm."

I closed my eyes for a moment. I knew how much he relished taunting me and I couldn't allow him to see my aggravation.

"Send her back to play in the mud!" one of the men called from behind Jaef. A ripple of badgering and laughter erupted within the group.

"Yeah, she's supposed to be the best Crawler... let her prove it!" another shouted over the tittering.

Jackasses. I scowled at them before dropping to my knees next to Jaef, who had bent down and been rifling through my haul.

"There's no more down there. Look, I can gather a whole lot more on my own if you just let me search the lake in my own way. I'll find us more, and that'll make you look good. You know I'll find lots."

His green eyes locked onto mine, his being the faded, dark color of last night's broccoli soup. In all fairness, he was only doing what he had been told by Sandor. Still, I hated being this close to him.

To my utter surprise, he gave me a quick, begrudging nod.

"Fine. Take your break and then move out on your own. I think you've played in enough mud for now."

I wanted to smile, but I didn't want to risk my satisfaction sparking another round of taunts from the goons, so I bit on my lip instead and thanked him before he could change his mind.

Despite the toxicity of it, I savored the pockets of clear water in the more remote corners of the lake. I scavenged a few of my more hidden dive holes and scored a bunch of cans brought in by a recent, strong undercurrent. I was stuffing my bag with scraps and feeling a growing pit in my stomach as I imagined the metal merchants dumping my haul on the piles where it would sit for years to come. I was going to make Jaef look like a genius, and I was doing what I loved, but I was slowly poisoning myself with this inner conflict.

After a few hours, I decided I'd more than met my quota for the day. I kicked through the water like a fish as I broke the surface for some air and a much-deserved break. As I paddled to the shore, I spotted that Corvax kid lingering along a knotted collection of trees by the edge of the woods.

I reached the embankment and faltered, deliberately taking my time to remove my Bright and goggles. What could he possibly want now? Hadn't his presence caused enough turmoil in my life? Did I really want to know?

His dark eyes scampered around the area like a frightened deer as he motioned me to come closer. He wasn't running off this time—he was seeking me out. My curiosity got the better of me.

I sighed and made my way over to him. I really did want to know what he wanted.

"What are you doing here?"

I wrang out my drenched braid, waiting for his answer. His lips looked like swollen plums as his face tightened.

"I have more to tell you."

The kid had been clutching a tree trunk as if he'd collapse without its support. I rolled my eyes and shook my head.

"Leave me alone. I've already gotten into enough trouble because of you. Go back into your hole."

"You don't understand. There are other things I need to show you."

My brow furrowed. "What things?"

"Stuff–secrets about the Crows."

I frowned. The last time I'd found out a Crow secret, Asher lost his hand.

"What secrets?"

He scowled at me.

"I can't show you now. Meet me at the tunnel at midnight tonight, and I'll reveal everything."

31

"How was your day, hon?" Grandpa asked as I settled in beside him for our last cup of tea for the evening.

"Alright."

"Did Jaef go easy on you?"

I thought about my morning dredge in the black mud.

"He was fine, Grandpa." I smiled.

"Good. At least you're crawling again. You always loved crawling, just like your father—your mother, too. They'd go together, you know."

My heart hollowed at the mention of my parents. The feeling was familiar, like an old companion haunting me.

"I know. They were a force together, right?"

His face went blank as he sipped on the herbal tea.

"Grandpa?"

He blinked slowly and cranked his head to look at me.

"Hmm? Oh, yes, at least you'll keep away from the Nest now. It's all for the best. No more trouble. No more death."

I frowned. Another familiar feeling crept up on me. The

feeling he was withholding information. Suddenly, the urge to find out became overwhelming.

"Who said anything about death?"

He shook his head vaguely, and his eyes swept to his lap.

"Death is a toll taker, waiting for us all at the border. Don't arrive too early. Stay alive. Don't make trouble."

"Are you talking about my father and the uprising?"

"Too early, his death came too early. And then it claimed your mother."

"Because he joined the push for our freedom, for a revolution? Some might say his death was righteous."

He turned on me with a spark in his faded eyes and scorn on his lips. I couldn't help but flinch.

"And some might say his death was in vain. The uprising changed nothing for Hydrans. Better to let things be because change will come in good time, all on its own."

"At least he fought for his beliefs."

"And paid with his life and that of your mother's, leaving you orphaned. Are beliefs worth that? You think the Crows will stop at taking Asher's hand? Wake up, girl."

I felt the burn in my cheeks. I wasn't a child anymore, but he seemed to forget that fact. I squared my jaw and fought to keep my voice steady.

"I'd rather die for my beliefs like my father than face a life of subservient misery. What are you hiding from me?"

He stood up at that, his crooked spine hunching him over toward me. I wanted to shrink away under the floor at my feet. I took a breath and braced myself for a lashing, but it never came. His temper dissolved as fast as it had emerged, and his face softened.

"He didn't just fight. He led the uprising against the Crows. When they were done putting down the rebellion, they came for your mother to make sure no other Hydrans would ever consider such a revolution again."

I stumbled. My father led it? And the Crows punished my mother for his actions? All these years later, and he'd just now decided to tell me this?

"What do you mean? I don't understand."

"You're a child of rebellion in more ways than one, my dear. Your father took up arms against the Crows, and they took his life for it. And then your mother's. It almost broke me, but I had you to look after."

Too much. My brain couldn't keep up, and my eyes drifted to the floor.

"Why don't I know about this? Nobody has ever talked about it."

"To do so would be treason. It has been forbidden."

His face softened as if that was all the explanation that was needed. My grandfather's calloused fingers brushed across my hand, startling me out of my thoughts. My face burned as I looked at him through watery eyes.

"I'm so proud of you, hon," he said, giving my hand a weak squeeze. "Your folks never had a chance against those Crows. They have weapons that we don't. I don't want you to end up like your father. Obey the rules, Rayna. Living in peace is better than losing everything."

"I need to tell you about something that I've seen. Something that is dangerous and could create a war. I need your help, Grandpa."

He sat down once more and leaned back in the chair with a tired sigh. His eyes became drowsy.

"Tomorrow, my dear. It can wait until tomorrow."

I watched him as his fingers loosened around his tea mug and sleep stole him away. His breath became heavy as I took the mug from him and tucked his blanket up under his chin.

"Yes. Tomorrow we'll talk and face the truth. We will *all* have to face the truth." I leaned in to kiss him on the cheek.

Then I quietly slipped from the hut to meet Shepherd.

32

The woods pulsed like a black mystery underneath the charcoal, night sky. The trees appeared spidery and brutal, the trail a deep brown path that led further into a world of unusual clicks and grunts. I told myself it was just the nighttime animals on their hunt and that, although the woods spread out like a blanket of ink, it was still the same place I'd have skipped through in the daylight. Even still, it took everything I had to keep putting one foot in front of the other. I couldn't stop the thump of my heart banging like a drum inside my chest.

I arrived at the mouth of the tunnel a few minutes early and waited. The silvery shine of the moon cast luminous shadows around the clearing. The air felt eerie and thick as I perched on a tall rock while sounds continued to fill my head—ones I'd only ever heard from a distance and the security of my bed. My breath quickened.

That kid better show up, and it better be soon.

My fingers began to twist furiously through my loosened hair, and by the time I was sure midnight was long past, I'd made several knots I knew I'd have to work at to unravel later. What was I doing? I'd just found out that it was my father who'd led the uprising and paid with his life—and it had cost my mother hers, as well. Why was I so bent on disobeying the rules? My grandfather's words began to ring in my mind on a relentless loop.

I leaped to my feet. The kid wasn't coming.

My boots dug into the moist earth as I swiveled to leave when a sudden noise stopped me in my tracks, and I whirled around to face the vines shielding the tunnel as Shepherd burst into view.

He doubled over, panting heavily.

"Rayna! Wait!" he said while trying to catch his breath. He held up a palm.

I stepped closer to him, his body distorted and ghostly against the backdrop of the thick vines.

"You're late."

"I know, I'm sorry. I think someone might've seen me leaving the Nest. I can't be sure."

He appeared to catch his breath, straightened up, and shoved a package at me.

"Here. Take this and run."

"Huh?"

Was this some kind of a joke? I hadn't risked coming all the way out here for some flimsy package.

He shook his head. His round eyes peered through the darkness like an owl then, and his voice quickened.

"There's no time. Everything you need to know is in there. Now, go. Please hurry!"

He nudged my shoulder with his left hand before turning around and vanishing through the vines.

My face twisted as my hands turned the package over several times. Other than the mysterious noises of the forest, I hadn't heard any other people approaching. But, clearly, he'd been afraid, so much so that he'd risked handing me something that I imagined could easily be traced back to him. I clutched the package to my chest and ran from the dark woods as fast as I could.

Why was I risking everything like my father?

Grandpa was right, I supposed. I was a child of rebellion. I was my father's daughter.

33

The early morning sun cast shadows on the Fremont Troll, his silhouette stretched over the graffiti-speckled walls. I sat with my legs folded beneath me and leaned against a stone toe, waiting for the fire I'd just started to catch. Shepherd's package lay loosely in my lap. My heartbeat slowed down to normal as I peered up at the Troll's face as if asking for his permission to open the package. He looked out across Freemont with his stony, eternal grin.

As I untwisted the last of the string and pulled it away from the layers of brown paper, the first thing I noticed was the musty, earthy odor wafting off the spine of what lay before me. I ran my fingers over the gilded lettering of the battered leather cover. Between these frayed pages, I sensed that many secrets had been hidden.

Why would the kid give this to me, a Hydran? It didn't make sense, but somehow, I knew that whatever this book revealed, it would change my life forever. Did I really want to know?

Hell. Yes.

When I unclipped the tarnished brass latch, the book sprang open in an avalanche of pages, one folded piece of paper falling into my lap. As I briefly flipped through the tome, I realized I held Shepherd's personal journal in my hands. And the folded paper that had fallen from the book was a hand-drawn map of the Nest.

Whoa.

I stopped right then and there and glanced up at the Troll. I knew I was alone, but it felt as though a set of accusatory eyes was on me, and it raised the hair on the back of my neck.

Pausing, I heard nothing but the gentle, crackling flames and the lake tide lapping against the shore.

I held up the map in the dawn's light while the fire warmed my face. I had been exhausted when I'd gotten to Freemont, but now my heart fluttered as I perused the detailed sketches of all the Nest's main locations, including Corvus' secret quarters where he'd hold his private cabinet meetings when away from the Needle. In jagged red ink, several entrances to the Nest had been clearly marked on the diagram, along with hidden passage-ways and obscure tunnels that cut across Queen Anne Hill, around the scrapyard, and even beneath the Nest. My hands trembled with the weight of this forbidden information as I thought about how these weaknesses could be exploited if one had enough people to do it. To start something. A rebellion.

The inked pages of the journal felt hot to the touch, or perhaps it was the unadorned pleasure of looking at something I knew was not for my eyes. I began to feel dizzy and over-whelmed with this burden of knowledge. I could barely believe what Shepherd had included in this journal as I read through the material, realizing he had spent hours gathering information on the Crows—his own people—and ultimately handed it to me.

It didn't make sense until I picked up that piece of paper that had fallen in my lap and saw that is was addressed to me. I read the hastily-scrawled note that looked as if it had been written while riding a horse. The more I read, the clearer it became.

Corvus had not only subjugated the Hydrans, but he'd abused

his own people and killed anyone who dissented, especially the Corvax Crows. The evidence had been well-documented in the pages of the journal—names, dates, and more. The kid had reached the breaking point. He wanted to bring Corvus down, but he hadn't been sure how a single Corvax Crow could possibly fight back against Lord Corvus and all his resources. Shepherd made it clear in his note that it was time to fight, but that the revolt had to be started by an outsider, someone not beholden to the social pressures and fear of loss that permeated the Nest. The information in the journal could be used to burn Queen Anne Hill to the ground. And it seemed as though he believed a Hydran would be the only way to ignite that fire. Shepherd needed an outsider. A rebel.

He needed me.

I sat by the fire for hours, devouring pages filled with text and diagrams. By the time my eyes began to grow too heavy to focus, I could feel exhaustion taking hold. I'd been on high alert through a lot the previous night and early that morning, and I decided to lay down next to the fire to rest for a moment before I went off to crawl for the day. As I drifted off into a fitful sleep, I became aware that perhaps I could no longer deny the path that stretched out before me. I had not chosen to receive the journal— the journal had chosen me—and Grandpa had always told me there was power in knowledge.

34

The chill woke me like a brittle shard of ice against my cheek. I jumped to awareness, my breath a misty white vapor mingling with the confusion. I sat upright and hugged my knees to my chest. I blinked a few times as everything from before rushed into my thoughts, and I remembered why I'd come to the Troll to be alone. My eyes fell upon Shepherd's journal. My head had started to spin again with all the future possibilities that the pages had created when something else hit me—I was supposed to be out crawling for Jaef.

Shit. If I were a no-show, it would raise all kinds of suspicions. I couldn't risk that happening.

I scrambled to grab my things, picking up the journal, rolling it back within the folds of the brown paper, and stringing it together like a mad woman. I stuffed it under my jacket and ran for the village as fast as my legs would carry me. At this time of the morning and with the little sleep I'd had, I was surprised at how fast I was able to run.

Almost there.

I'd hide the journal under my mattress, grab my diving gear, and get to the lake. I could make it before Jaef became too dubious, I was sure.

I skirted the fields and the long, leafy stalks of corn. The village came into view as I rounded the trail and almost collided with Lyra. Her long, auburn hair flamed under the rising sun, her freckled nose scrunched up tight.

"Rayna! Where have you been? I've been searching for you everywhere."

"Why now? I need to get to the lake. I'm already late." I inched away from her, but she grabbed my shoulders, her nails digging into my flesh as her hazel eyes found mine.

"No, you have to get home. Something has happened."

"What?"

Suddenly, my body shivered. My arms and legs tingled lightly, even feeling a little agitated.

"What happened? Tell me—is it Asher?"

She dropped her hands from my shoulders and began linking her fingers in a twist, while her eyes fell somewhere around my ankles. She began to shake her head.

"I...I—Rayna, just go home, okay?"

My mouth became dry, my tongue sticking to my lips. Something had happened, and even fast-talker Lyra wouldn't tell me.

"Go home, Rayna."

I whirled about and dashed toward my house while trying not to let my imagination take me to a dark place. When I got home, though, I'd realize that I didn't need a vivid imagination to do that—life could handle that all on its own.

35

*I*t was as if I were caught in a nightmare, but I knew I was awake. The sun rose higher in the sky, and the birds continued to sing as they soared in the morning light. My feet moved me through the village streets, and I walked like a shadow of myself. When I saw the people milling around outside my house, a cold feeling clenched my stomach and reminded me that this was all real.

My feet slowed as I got closer, my heart stuttering as I saw the sorrow on the faces of the people outside my home, their eyes wet and downcast. I felt the burn of tears in my own eyes as heads dropped when I passed by.

What had happened? I had no idea, but at the same time, I knew exactly what had occurred. I quickened my pace. I had to see for myself.

I burst through the door and stumbled as I took in the scene. The room was quiet, the fire smoldering in the far corner and Grandpa sitting in his rocking chair with his quilt tucked under his chin, just as I'd left him the night before. The village doctor was kneeling beside him, and Ember hovered over him on the other side, tears glistening on her cheeks as she glanced my way.

"Oh, Rayna. They've finally found you. When you didn't show up at the lake this morning, one of the Crawlers entered your home and found him. Like this…"

My eyes focused on my grandfather. I knew why he was still sitting in his chair at this time of the morning. I knew why he'd not berated me for staying out all night or coming back to the hut instead of crawling. And I knew why the village doctor was inside our home.

"Grandpa!"

I staggered to my knees, my head scrambling as I looked at his face. His mouth gaped open, his lips tinged blue and his open eyes glassy and distant. I reached for his hand—his skin was cold, his fingers rigid.

"No!"

I buried my face in his shoulder and cried. My body shook. I vaguely heard Ember's soft, comforting words behind me as she stroked my back.

I was alone. All alone.

I stifled a sob as I clutched at his lifeless hand, pressing my lips against his skin and kissing it.

"Oh, Grandpa."

The doctor tried saying something to me, but my devastation had sucked the noise from the room and my vision blurred through a veil of tears. I didn't want to hear what he had to say. I knew all I needed to know.

"I'm so sorry, Rayna. There was nothing I could do. We found him this way…"

His words were muffled as he spoke. I wanted him to shut up. I wanted him to leave.

I felt numb as I looked back at Grandpa and ran my fingers through his wiry grey hair. He had become a stranger already, the physical form before me no longer resembling the grandpa I had loved. He was gone.

I kissed him on the cheek and whispered in his ear. "I'm sorry, Grandpa. I'm sorry for not listening to you. I love you so much."

I should have been a better granddaughter. I could have done better. I could have stayed out of the Nest, stopped asking questions, and obeyed the rules. Grief and guilt spiraled through me like a remorseful coil as my world felt shattered. I collapsed into Ember's waiting arms and sobbed.

Her fingers caressed my hair, and she murmured into my ear. "It'll be okay. He's at peace now. He'll always be with you."

Her words made my heart ache and I held her tighter, feeling lost and void. There was no end to the flood of cascading tears. I didn't even notice Chief Sandor when he walked into the room, but I felt his strong hand brush across my shoulders.

"I'm sorry for your loss."

I took the handkerchief Ember offered me and sniffled into the folded fabric before acknowledging Sandor with a blank nod.

Grandpa was gone. I couldn't even muster a respectful response to our village leader.

"You may take the day off from crawling to mourn and make funeral preparations."

Funeral preparations? How could I even think about preparing anything right now, let alone Grandpa's funeral? I didn't want to think about it.

Ember pulled me back into her warm embrace and peered at Sandor over my head.

"She will come home with me. The villagers will tend to him and make the proper preparations."

Thank goodness for Ember.

"Very well," Sandor said, glancing at me again. "I'm sure you're in good hands."

I could only nod as he turned and walked from the room.

36

_T_he bleak morning light invaded my room through the cracks in the wall. I pulled the blanket over my eyes and rolled over, wishing to fall back asleep rather than face the day. The world felt strange now that Grandpa was gone, and I wasn't sure how'd I'd get through it. How do you adjust when the man who raised you leaves you behind?

A heavy sigh escaped my lips, and I felt the fresh well of tears begin to brim.

Being honest with myself, I knew his death had been inevitable. His mental and physical condition had begun to deteriorate rapidly in the past few months, and he had lived a long life. But sometimes it was better to live in sweet ignorance than deal with the bitter truth.

Our last conversation replayed in my mind. He had told me to, "wake up, girl" and he knew how much I hated it when he called me that. It made me feel small and powerless. I hadn't the chance to tell him what I saw at the Kerry Park Scrapyard, knowing his years of wisdom would have been so valuable.

I sat up and threw my blanket aside, swinging my feet to the cold floor. I guessed I really was powerless. I was "just a girl." I didn't know where to go or what to do.

As I wandered through the empty hut, everything reminded me of him. His rocking chair still sat by the fireplace, his frayed quilt folded neatly over one arm. But it was when I saw his mud-caked boots by the door that I caved. I picked them up and held them to my chest, the dried dirt flaking out over my night clothes and sprinkling to the floor. They smelled like the fields, and they felt like an old friend. I sobbed as I clung to a belonging that had been so important to him.

I felt as if I had somehow failed my grandfather. I should have been there at the end, to hold his hand and ease him into his transition. Instead, I had chosen to meet with Shepherd against Grandpa's wishes, and I hadn't been there when he'd needed me the most. All his advice maneuvered through my head like a floating jigsaw puzzle. I seemed to have always resisted his guidance. Why was I such a stubborn ass? I was sure I had let him down. Just like I'd let Asher down. The feeling began to overtake me. I had to make things right.

I went back to my room, slumped on my bed, and pulled out Shepherd's journal. I flipped through the pages without seeing a thing and wondered if the information contained in these pages held the solution to righting the wrongs of our society. My mind filled with the familiar flicker of loathing as I contemplated how I could best use the wisdom in the journal. Grandpa wanted me to obey, to play it safe. And yet, the Crows had taken everything from me. Maybe if Grandpa had been given access to better medicine, maybe he'd still be around—but that medicine was all hoarded in the Nest.

His sweet voice played in my head like a relentless melody, his words stirring inside of me. I shook my head, trying to reconcile his suggestion that I conform with my desire to right the wrongs of generations, to make sure my parents hadn't died in vain.

I stuffed the journal away and set about getting dressed before brewing some fresh tea.

The time passed slowly that grey day. Each minute came with growing anxiety that I tried to repress without succeeding. By the time the expected knock at the door came, my fingers ached from the constant fiddling. I rose from the chair, my movements mechanical as I opened the door to the woman who told me it was time.

I stepped from my home and followed her, feeling as if I were gliding between myself and someplace else I'd rather be—which at that point was anywhere but there. It was time for the village to say farewell to my grandfather and wish him safe passage into the next world. And I knew I had to somehow keep breathing.

37

The soft candlelight glowed upon Ember's face as she smiled at me. Her eyes glazed over, and I could see she was barely holding everything back.

"You look beautiful."

I looked down at myself. A handful of village women had dressed me in an ivory gown for the ceremony. The delicate fabric brushed against my skin. It felt delicate and supple as its folds flowed over my curves and cinched in at my waist. A twisted head wreath adorned my forehead; the white flowers had been freshly handpicked and made a striking contrast against my dark hair.

I sighed. I had never felt so feminine. The feeling was as disturbing as it was enchanting. Was this how women in the Nest felt? I guessed I would never know. I wished my grandfather could see me now. He had never seen me dressed this way and I knew he would have liked it. How ironic that it was all for him.

"Are you ready to see him?" Ember asked, watching me closely.

I shrugged. "I guess."

Hydrans held funerals at night. They placed the body on a raft with wildflowers, stones, and feathers, surrounded by an arrangement of wood. The Chief would then set the raft on fire and push it into Elliot Bay with blessings for a safe journey to the afterworld. It was believed that burning the bodies released them from any earth-bound human attributes that might otherwise linger, giving them a clean slate to enter the next life.

They had my grandfather in a small hut by the lake where they prepared the dead for their final journey. Ember and Asher walked on either side of me, each of my hands twisted through theirs as we entered the room. My grandfather's body lay stretched along a timber slab, ready to be carried to the raft waiting by the shore. He was covered from the neck down in a swathe of thin white cheesecloth, and stones concealed his eyes, lending him sight for his voyage.

A lump wedged firmly in my throat as I turned to Asher and his mother.

"May I have a moment alone with him?"

They nodded and left me alone with my grandfather for the last time.

When I turned back to look at him, despair crippled my heart and torment ripped through my mind. I stepped closer, noting how his skin was grey and pasty, his whiskers stiff on his chin. How many times had I pulled on those whiskers as a child? Too many times to count. I wanted to tug on them again and hear his laughter as he tickled me back. But those times had been forever lost to the past, and the enormity of his death rumbled through me like a storm cloud.

I buckled at the knees and hugged him. I cried until my eyes were raw and my ribs ached. I sobbed and wished for one last embrace. One last "I love you." So, I cupped his stark chin in my hands and kissed his cheek and told him how much I loved him. This was my last goodbye to the man I'd cherished my whole life, and afterward it took every bit of strength I had to turn and walk away from him.

I left the room and came face to face with Sandor. He was waiting outside with Ember and Asher, and he approached me right away with his hands outstretched. His sober face gazed down at me as his large hands clasped my own.

"Your grandfather was a well-respected man, Rayna. His loss will be felt by us all. The whole village has come to bid him farewell. You have all of my heartfelt condolences."

I felt drained when I looked into Sandor's eyes. My mind was a haze, like the mist that clung to the lake in the mornings. I just wanted to get this over with now.

"Thank you."

He nodded and turned away, his white robes flowing behind him. It was time for him to bless the body by the shore and push the pyre into the bay.

The gritty sand crunched under my feet, but I didn't notice. I didn't see the faces gathered around. I didn't hear the voices, nor the cries, nor the usual blessing the Chief gave to the dead as he enthroned their last sacred journey. All I saw was the moon ascending on the horizon, and the flames carried away by the tide with my grandfather's body slowly disintegrating between them.

The breeze blew and whipped around my face. Strands of hair stuck to my lips and my eyes, yet I continued to stand at the shore and watch my grandfather sail away into the night forever. Asher stood silently next to me as the villagers began to shamble away and return to their huts. My friend stood firm even when the rain began to fall, and I could no longer distinguish between my tears and the shower that drenched us.

I felt unraveled. Undone. I was unclear about the future, and my thoughts became erratic as the raft disappeared, my grandfather's body leaving this earth. A word drifted through the downpour and into my ears.

"Rayna."

It was Asher. His smooth, calming voice encapsulated me. I

blinked and looked up at him. His hair stuck to his forehead like brown cement, his long lashes glistening.

"Let's go home."

I nodded and entwined my hand with his, and walked through the desolate village feeling like a lost soul drenched in darkness.

———————

38

*M*y eyes passed over the Crawlers while I stood on the shore of Lake Union and watched them begin their day's work. Grey clouds hovered low and ominous, threatening another downpour. I'd used to think that it couldn't rain forever, but I didn't know anymore. The air swirled around all of us, chilling my bones with a heavy blanket of fog. Yet, still, the Crawlers strapped on their gear and trekked into the filthy water one by one, the tired look of routine etched across their faces.

What were we doing out here? Day after miserable day, we slaved, doing our best to meet the aluminum quota set by Corvus. And for what? Nothing.

I couldn't get the image out of my mind. Heaps and heaps of aluminum at the top of Queen Anne Hill. Scraps of rations in our village below. These men and women—the Crawlers and other people in the fields—they toiled their entire lives to end up on a burning raft in Elliot Bay. What was the point?

Shepherd's journal flashed through my mind. I had concealed it in a watertight bag and brought it along with me. For some reason, keeping the journal close eased the restlessness turning in my mind and gave me a sense of comfort. Or perhaps it was the impression of power the book evoked in me that I liked. I just had to figure out what I was going to do with the information and I didn't want to risk leaving it in a place where others might find it—at least not until I had decided what to do with the journal.

I sighed and pulled on my Bright and goggles, each movement filled with a new hostility. And by the time I'd finished, I'd nearly taken off a handful of my own hair. I wanted to scream. I wanted to summon the Crawlers back to the shore and tell them to go home to their families. I wanted to burn—to feel raw, unadulterated pain. To lash out and scream for justice. My own self-directed anger started to rise like a Tsunami, an imminent eruption over so many wrongs I had lived with for so long.

Why should the Crows deserve a better life than the Hydrans? What made them so superior, standing above us both figuratively and literally? Suddenly, the thought of crawling filled me with an immense emptiness, a frustrating sense of futility over something I'd spent my entire life doing, something that had once filled me with pride.

All these thoughts swam through my mind, and I lost track of where I was and what I was doing. I didn't hear Jaef as he came up beside me.

"Rayna?"

I jerked so hard, I almost shed my skin. I turned on him fast, a dark glare glinting my eyes.

"What?"

He looked at me with his head down, his shoulders slumped. Then, Jaef gave me his best impersonation of a smile.

"Are you okay?" His voice had cracked on the question as he'd kicked at the clumpy sand.

I glowered at him. "I don't need your pity."

His eyes skirted to his feet, the corners of his mouth drooped.

"I just wanted to make sure you—"

"I'm fine." I felt my face flush, and I looked past Jaef as a

Crawler's head broke the surface of the water with a half-filled sack on his back.

"Are you sure?"

"Just because I lost my grandfather doesn't mean you have to pretend to like me. Leave me alone. I have a job to do. You of all people should know that."

I whirled around and swooped up my bag. Just the sight of Jaef's face made me want to hurl. As if he had ever cared about me or my feelings before. Phony.

The wind gusted again, now shifting and coming from the north where the cold, mountain winds emerged from the frozen peaks. I'd often dreamt of hiking into the Cascades and leaving everything behind. With Grandpa gone, I'd started to question exactly what "everything" really meant.

I stomped into the murky lake just as the rain began to fall. But it did nothing to extinguish the angry fire now burning inside of me. I stuffed my snorkel between my teeth and dove down into the depths of the dark lake.

---

39

*I*t had been off limits for a long time. Maybe even going back to my grandfather's time. Crawlers had always warned each other of dangerous holes, but at the same time, I knew that sometimes they'd also just warn of danger in order to keep out competition.

I kicked hard and pushed through the water, seeing the dangling, tattered piece of red cotton that had marked the under-water cave. It wasn't a natural cave, more like a cavern created by a lot of old junk left over from the old times—steel barrels, car doors, etc.

The soft current pulled me into the entrance, and I looked over my shoulder, mistakenly thinking I was alone. I'd wish later that I would have looked harder.

After ten or fifteen minutes of crawling, rising to the surface for air and dropping down again, I'd decided that either the cave was dangerous as marked, or more likely, it had been crawled out.

The bubbles in the water were my first clue.

Jaef probably sent the kid to follow me, and now here he was, twisting his face beneath the goggles and gesturing toward the cave. I shook my head, but he ignored me and swam inside.

As I think back now, I really don't know what happened to that kid. I didn't give him much thought and swam to the surface where I saw Jaef pointing at me. I rolled over and swam the backstroke toward the shore as I heard more voices. I was within 50 yards of Jaef when I knew something was wrong.

Jaef and the rest of his crew were jumping up and down like idiots, and once I came out of the lake and knocked the water from my ears, I realized what they were saying.

"He's still down there!"

The moron who'd followed me hadn't come up, and I knew that meant he was probably trapped beneath the debris, which must have shifted. Whoever had put that piece of cloth over the entrance had known that someday that pile would collapse. Today was that day.

Jaef dove into the water and kicked past me before I realized what he was doing. He dropped beneath the surface with a 1-2 kick of his legs and a splash of water. The guy couldn't find aluminum in the middle of the Kerry Park Scrapyard, and yet he apparently thought he'd be able to rescue the other guy in water that was at least a good fifty yards from the shore—and probably stuck in that cave.

I debated diving, too, but by the time I'd mentally made the decision, Jaef broke the surface with his arm around the kid's shoulder. As he dragged the boy through the water, the rest of Jaef's crew rushed over and pulled them both onto the cold, dirty sand.

"Thanks for nothing."

As the water cascaded off my body and I stomped through the ankle-deep water, I realized Jaef was talking to me. I found out later that the kid had gotten his foot caught in some debris. He had freaked out and pulled it loose just as Jaef dove down and reached him.

"You were treading above the hole. All you had to do was exhale and kick down."

"I'm not your babysitter." I felt bad talking about the kid who had almost drowned, but I couldn't hold my frustration back. "Next time, send someone who knows better than to go crawling in a flagged hole."

"Next time, maybe you oughta stay out of those areas, too."

I turned my back on Jaef with a dismissive wave. Whatever. I wasn't the one who'd had to be pulled out of the water, gagging and half-drowned. It seemed like yet another example of just how useless Jaef was. I cursed under my breath, thinking that I wouldn't have been all that upset if *he'd* been the one trapped in the cave.

After going through my post-crawl routine and gathering my stuff, I reached for my bag. Damn. I should have been more careful.

"What's that?" Jaef asked from five feet behind me. "Is that your girly diary?"

"It's nothing." I tried shoving Shepherd's journal back into my bag, but as they say, it was already out.

"Let me see it."

"No, Jaef. It's none of your business."

The others had circled around me, even the kid who had almost drowned. He seemed to be fully recovered, grinning like a fool as Jaef kept picking at me.

"I said, let me see it."

"And I said *no*."

I didn't know if Jaef moved on me or if one of his jerks pushed him, but he barreled into me and almost knocked me over. I dropped the journal and it hit the sand with a flat, wet pop. Everybody stood frozen, as it had landed face up, the embossed leather cover proudly displaying the Mark of the Crow.

"Rayna, Rayna."

Jaef bent down and snatched it before I could. The other Crawlers stepped between us.

"Thanks for letting me take a look. You guys all saw her throw the journal at me, right?"

I felt the heat on my cheeks, and I'd curled my fingers into fists before I realized that my heartbeat had jumped, and my mouth became dry. I took one step forward, and that's when it started.

Shouting and screams came from the village. And although we were too far away to hear what people were saying, we heard enough to know that it wasn't a celebration. Something was happening. Something bad.

Two of Jaef's crew started running, and he looked at me. "This ain't over."

I ran at him, but the kid who'd almost drowned stepped in front of Jaef, striking me from the side and knocking me off balance. I stumbled back and fell into the lake. When I sat up and wiped the burning water from my face, I could see the back of Jaef as he ran to the village along with the other Crawlers.

When I scanned the sand, I saw my open bag and my gear scattered on the dirty sand, but Shepherd's journal wasn't there.

I didn't know whether to run to the village or dive back down into the water and let the cavern collapse upon me, too.

40

*I*t felt as though the ancient ground under my boots had started sliding toward the sea. The world as I'd known it sat on the edge of an unknown ocean, dragging us all out in a dangerous riptide.

The entire village had gathered in the square, and an army of Crow soldiers patrolled the area like trained guard dogs. My head spun as I realized that, whatever had happened, it couldn't possibly be good if it required armed guards.

I snaked through the crowd, the pit of my stomach cramped in a tight stitch as the rumbling among the people faded into light murmurs. A loud voice broke over the square. Thanks to my lithe frame, I'd managed to sneak my way toward the front, where I saw Aren. And, in front of him, the man himself, Lord Corvus.

He stood tall and erect in his black cloak and matching pants while his icy eyes surveyed the crowd. He didn't say a word, but he didn't need to. His hardened features and cold disposition conveyed his displeasure at being among Hydran people. He sniffed at the air, crinkling his nose and removing a folded handkerchief from his coat pocket. He turned toward his advisors who had arrived on horseback, flicking his handkerchief open and dabbing the sweat from his forehead.

"I am Lord Corvus, supreme leader of the Crows, regent of the Lowlands."

He paused and turned his head, probing the crowd with his frigid stare. Corvus wanted to impress us with his words, but even without knowing them, his point was perfectly clear—things were about to get a lot worse.

"A Crow traitor has been exposed, and a conspiracy revealed. An informer has been captured, and we believe he has been aiding a Hydran with confidential information about the Nest."

My heart almost stopped in my chest.

A frantic chatter raced through the square. Lord Corvus spoke over the commotion while Crow soldiers cracked their whips. I flinched as the sharp snaps cut through the air.

"Since we cannot be sure which Hydran among you has been in league with our snitch, and this regrettable event has occurred in quick succession after the last betrayal which Regent Aren so dutifully processed, I have decided the Hydran village itself will suffer the consequences instead of our identifying the perpetrator. And I can assure you, ladies and gentlemen, I do not have an inexhaustible supply of patience."

The man smiled as he gazed out at the crowd, his chest out and his head held high in anticipation of leveling self-righteous retribution. Silence fell upon the Hydrans as he turned and stabbed a gloved finger toward a string of horses milling behind the stage.

"Bring out the boy."

My muscles stiffened, my feet rooted into the ground. I couldn't run, and yet I thought that a gust off the lake would knock me over. Time slowed momentarily as I caught sight of Shepherd being led out by a Crow soldier. His narrow wrists had been bound, his milky complexion marred by congealed blood and swollen, blackened eyes. While he stumbled to collect his footing, the soldier yanked him along by pulling at the end of a rope looped around his slender neck.

My eyes stung while the crowd exploded and pushed around me, everyone trying to get a better view of whatever was about to happen. Crow soldiers cursed and lashed their whips into the air as a warning to the frenzied group. Corvus had come to our village to punish one of his own in front of us. I couldn't remember this ever happening before, and the thought of what would happen next made my stomach sour.

Corvus gave us a long smirk as he watched the upheaval. When the crowd quietened, he cleared his throat and spoke again.

"The guilty party may appear young and innocent to you, but his rebellious flare has proven to be detrimental to both our societies, threatening the very system that sustains us all. I hereby sentence you, Corvax Crow, to death."

I froze. Shouts arose from all around me. I couldn't think—my head scrambled with thoughts going in all directions. I watched as a Crow soldier tugged on the sleeve of Shepherd's soiled garment. He collapsed into the dirt and staggered to get to his knees. He lifted his chin and peered through watery eyes at the crowd, and then at me, as the soldier pulled out a long, dirty blade and stepped behind him.

I cried out, my hands over my mouth. There hadn't been an execution in my lifetime, and certainly never a Crow. And a child at that. For a split second, I made eye contact with Shepherd, and in the boy's eyes, I saw forgiveness. And something more. Fury. He held my stare, and at that moment, I understood what he had communicated to me.

The soldier didn't hesitate. He slid the blade across the boy's throat, drawing a crimson line on his neck that let loose a river of blood. Shepherd gasped, and his eyes shot open before he toppled over and bled out into the dark, cold mud.

For the barest of moments, a strange feeling fell upon the

crowd. Restlessness? Terror? Grim satisfaction? I wasn't sure, but I couldn't really grasp the stark reality of Shepherd's execution, either. We didn't care much about what happened to the Crows or how Corvus ruled them, but the visceral shock of watching a young boy murdered before your eyes was not something easily processed. My initial thought was sadness for Shepherd followed by a cramp in my stomach and a cold sweat—if that was how much Corvus valued his own kind, what would he do to us?

We didn't have to wait long to find out.

Smoke.

It drifted on the cold wind and filled my lungs. I looked up to the sky and saw a black cloud over the village.

"And now for *your* punishment. Half of the fields have been torched—the half used to grow your crops. You will continue to farm and provide food for the Nest from the remaining half. Hydrans must venture into the forests to hunt or forage for anything else. And if that doesn't seem fair to you, I'd be happy to burn down the entire village instead."

I looked around and saw the realization on the faces of my fellow villagers. The lack of fresh crops. Venturing into the dangerous, dark forests. And, all the while, giving the Nest what we needed for the barest rations to survive and be spared Corvus' wrath.

One man spoke up from the crowd. "The forests are filled with wild animals and cursed creatures. And there isn't enough there to feed our entire village."

Corvus turned in the direction of the man who'd spoken. "You seem to be a clever, conniving sort. I'm sure you'll figure it out."

He stepped down from the stage, smiling, and headed toward his carriage with the soldiers in tow. Aren mounted his horse as the soldiers did the same, all of them galloping off without another word.

The villagers began to scatter—some toward the burning

fields, others heading for the safety of their huts. Thick smoke filling my lungs, the cruel, tantalizing scent of burning corn accompanying a dark rain of ash.

My knees shook as I approached Shepherd's lifeless body in the dirt at the base of the platform in the village square. Hydrans walked past him without a pause or a second look.

I wanted to stop and at least cover the boy's body, but the crowd nudged me in the other direction. Looking back a few moments later, I'd understand that that might have saved my life, as I saw Aren astride his horse at the top of the hill overlooking the Lowlands—no doubt waiting to see if anyone came to Shepherd.

Like a cold ocean wave, I let the flow of Hydran villagers pull me away from the grisly scene. I stopped in a deserted alley, no longer able to hold back my tears.

I cried for myself and my people as well as for Shepherd. I wanted to return home then, until I remembered that nothing but an empty hut waited for me.

No family. No food. No future.

41

I'd hung my head for so long that the nerves in my neck began to pinch and the muscles across my back felt heavy and ached, all as my blood charged with the desperate ring of despondency. Nothing was right anymore. I dropped my eyes back to my feet. I didn't care about the nagging pain clenching my body—at least I felt something. I was better off than Shepherd.

The villagers had taken to the narrow streets with people rushing about in pointless chaos. I listened as mothers screamed at children and men shouted at each other beneath the charred air. Few people bothered with the fields, realizing that the fire had consumed everything by now.

I sat there in that alley, unable to get up and yet feeling the restless energy in my stomach. I could go back to the hut. But then what? Would I be crawling tomorrow, or would Sandor send me out into the vast, dark wilderness to hunt? Maybe that would be for the better. Maybe I deserved it.

"There she is!"

I turned around to see Jaef pointing at me, Sandor's guards

standing in the street behind him. They ran past the jerk and grabbed me by the arms, yanking me to my feet.

"What the hell?"

The guard on my left gave me a stony stare. "Chief Sandor wants to see you."

My eyes flew to Jaef. He had led them to me, and at that moment, staring at his rotten face, I figured out why. He'd been the one to take the journal from my belongings, and he'd taken it to Sandor.

Bastard.

With physical evidence provided by Jaef, Sandor wouldn't be able to protect me any longer.

"You're nothing but a filthy rat."

He shrugged as the guard began to haul me away and I stumbled while trying to keep my eyes on Jaef.

"I'm doing what's right." Jaef waved at the destruction. "Look what you've done to our village!"

I yanked my arm hard, managing to dislodge it from the soldier's grip.

"I can walk on my own." I turned to face Jaef. "You have no idea what's right. What's just. You're a slave without chains—we all are."

"It's all your fault. You need to pay for what you've done."

I scowled as Sandor's guards yanked at my arms and dragged me through the village, my mind whirling like a thunderstorm.

As we approached Sandor's house, I could barely contain the rage boiling inside of me. I wanted to rip the hair from Jaef's stupid head and beat him bloody.

I toppled forward through the door as one the guards gave me a firm shove inside.

"Why, Rayna?"

Sandor's question felt pointless, and I honestly didn't have an answer for him. I lifted my chin and straightened my shoulders as I turned my head and made eye contact with our leader. Jaef stood behind me. I couldn't see him, but I could feel his slimy, oily presence. He could try being contrite, but I just knew the vermin was enjoying ratting me out.

"Why what?" I asked with a sneer, offering what was more like a statement of defiance rather than a question back to him.

For what felt like the longest time, Sandor just sat there staring at me.

"If you're repentant, I might be able to spare your life."

The lie burst forth, and I didn't even care. "I didn't do anything."

Sandor shook his head, and I heard Jaef huff behind me. The Chief's eyes moved to the table where Shepherd's journal sat, the Mark of the Crow staring at us all like a cruel, unblinking eye.

"Please don't make this harder than it has to be."

42

"It's all her fault, Chief! Asher, the extra aluminum quota, and now our fields are burning." Jaef threw his arms into the air in frustration, emphasizing his point.

As if that was necessary. I gave Jaef an indignant stare and inched away from him.

Sandor simply gazed down at the journal.

"What do you have to say for yourself?"

"What is there to say? She had a Crow journal. It's right there," Jaef said, stepping forward.

Sandor's thick lips thinned with his frown.

"I wasn't talking to you."

Jaef sighed, and opened his mouth to say something more before catching the glower on Sandor's face. Jaef snapped his jaw shut.

I suppressed a smirk, stifling any lingering satisfaction when Sandor directed his glare at me. The air in my lungs felt thick.

"Rayna, please say something that I can take to Corvus, something that might sound apologetic enough to save your life."

"If I tell you the truth, explain to you what I've seen, things will never be the same. For any of us."

Sandor's fierce stare held, and he waited, not immediately jumping in and demanding an apology. I took a hesitant step forward and motioned to the journal.

"That journal is not what you should be worried about. The real danger is sitting behind the walls of the Kerry Park Scrapyard."

Jaef's head turned sideways, my words leaving him silent—for once. Sandor sighed and crossed his arms over his chest.

"What are you talking about?"

Believe me when I say that telling Sandor about the heaps of wasted aluminum was the last thing I wanted to do. I had no way of knowing how entangled he'd become with Corvus. But I'd held it in for so long that I felt like the secret had begun eating away at me, a mental parasite weakening my willpower. Before I could make the decision, the words came rushing out.

"It's all a lie. They don't do anything with our hauls. Corvus forces a quota upon us so we'll keep busy and not realize how shitty our lives are compared to those in the Nest."

Jaef huffed, but Sandor's eyes didn't blink. He seemed to be staring right through me.

"She's a liar. Why would they do that? It doesn't make sense."

I shot Jaef a deadly look. I'd had enough of his crap to last me a lifetime.

"I admit to being in the Nest and having the journal. And Asher took the fall for me before I could do anything about it. I hid all of that. But I'm telling you the truth about the aluminum. We risk our lives crawling for nothing. We work our hands raw in the fields or at the bottom of the lake and exchange that toil for puny, rotten vegetables while the lowest of the Crows eat bacon in the Nest. *Bacon.*"

"Silence!"

Sandor rose to his feet, the chair scraping over the wooden floor.

I'd immediately shut my mouth, but couldn't keep from adding, "Chief, I'm sorry, but I can't live this lie anymore."

"Save your apologies for Lord Corvus, who I am sure will be returning to interrogate the Hydran responsible for this debacle."

"What do you mean?"

He took strides around the table, and came so close to me that I didn't know where to look. My eyes flitted up to him.

"I must deliver him the guilty party, or he will take further action against our village. You're going to prison until I can decide how to handle this whole mess."

Ever the politician, Sandor had sidestepped my revelation, skillfully hiding his emotional response to it.

"I don't care. I've been living in one."

"Oh, you will, you disrespectful, arrogant bitch. How dare you place me in this kind of predicament? Forced to hand over one of my own to spare the rest of this village—even if that person is an insubordinate, lying troublemaker."

He looked beyond me and called for his guards. My stomach lurched, and my head felt foggy as Sandor turned his back on me and walked away. My legs buckled as the guards dragged me from the room. I could hear Jaef snickering.

43

It wasn't long before I knew every inch of the bleak prison walls surrounding me. I fast discovered the thing about being locked away in prison wasn't so much that I couldn't walk freely or inhale the fresh air at will—it was the isolation that drove me insane. I was left to ponder. Left to peel back all the layers and confront my innermost feelings. And I found myself riding these emotional waves that surged through me at disturbing speeds.

The cold springs of the cot bit into my ribs as I lay on my side, watching a cockroach crawl around in search of food.

"There's nothing here for you."

There was nothing there for me, either. I felt empty, and at that moment, I could care less about Sandor's plans for my future. I stared at the insect now sharing my cell, and I thought about its simple existence. Was life meant to be this complicated and troublesome? Or was it me who had attracted all this turmoil? Should I have listened to my grandfather and followed the rules?

A grinding noise shook me from my depressing reflections. I

sat up on the cot and saw a guard emerging from the light of the opened door and coming down the stairs toward my cell.

He stopped just short of my cage and gave me a cold stare.

"You have a visitor." The man had spit out the words, his tone hardened steel that was no different than the bars surrounding me.

But I took no notice of that as I saw Asher push past him and come into view. I leaped to my feet and approached the locked door, smiling before I realized I was even doing it.

"Hi, Asher."

His blue eyes swam as he teared up, and I wanted nothing more than to pull him to my heart and hold him tightly. He stuck his hand between the bars.

"That kid gave the information to you, didn't he?"

I looked down at his hand and nodded as I grasped it. I wound my fingers around his and squeezed. We'd both known the truth when the Crows had shown up and executed Shepherd. Still, Asher needed to hear it from me. When I looked back at him, his eyes shone with tears.

"Oh, Asher. Everything will be okay, I just know it."

He shook his head slowly, tears now falling freely. I guessed he'd reached his breaking point. How much more could this poor guy endure?

"You don't know that. They've put you in prison. What if Corvus kills *you*? If they're executing their own…"

I felt that defiant flame inside of me burning hotter. I clenched my jaw.

"I deserve to be here, but I'm not going to die," I said with more conviction than I felt. I had to ease his torment.

He took a breath, and I could see him mustering all his strength to gain control of his own feelings. His face twisted, and he grumbled something before asking me the next question.

"Did you go back into the Nest?"

"No. Shepherd gave me a journal filled with all sorts of information about the Crows and a detailed map of the Nest." I lowered my voice and leaned closer to the bars. "I know all of the secret passageways into the Nest–I know everything."

I couldn't tell him about the aluminum. He would be safer not knowing the truth.

His face darkened as he scowled and pulled his hand back through the bars.

"Forget about it! Information like that will get you killed! You need to stop all this, Rayna, and you need to stop it now. Give up the fight and stay alive, for God's sake. I need you to stay alive."

"There's something else," I said, watching him closely. "So much that's been hidden from us, holding us down and keeping us locked in an invisible prison."

Asher shook his head and wiped the tears from his face. He paused for a moment and then the words came in a whispered rush.

"I'm not interested in your cryptic conspiracy theories. Quit stirring up trouble and obey the laws of the Lowlands. I know this is wrong—Corvus, Sandor, our situation with the Crows. Deep down, we all know it. But standing against them is going to get you killed. If you agree to stop this, then I'm sure Sandor can talk to Corvus and spare your life. You'll be punished, but you won't be killed."

"Is that supposed to make me feel better?"

"No. It's meant to keep you alive. Don't end up like your father."

I stepped back until I could feel the cold, cell wall. I leaned against it to lower the temperature of my rising anger.

"My father stood up for what he believed. He gave his life for what's right. I see that now. The elders. This village. They might be embarrassed by the rebellion he led, but I'm not ignoring the truth any longer. I'm not pretending what my parents did was anything less than honorable. They were heroes."

"Heroes?" Asher folded his arms in front of his chest. "More like traitors. They ignored law and order. They started a war. I know that not everything is perfect, but at least we're alive. It could be worse."

"Could it, Asher? Look at the bandage on the end of your arm. Look where we're talking. Go look at our crops or the scrapyard we've died to fill. You don't think that's bad enough?"

He shook his head and stepped closer to the bars, reaching through again. I pushed off the wall and walked to the edge of the cell until Asher's hand caressed the side of my face. My eyes closed at his touch, my skin tingling with a stirring of emotions moving so quickly I could barely breathe.

"What will you do?"

I opened my eyes and stared hard into his.

"I don't know. Some things can't be ignored." My voice cracked as my heart opened and the truth flowed forth. "This isn't the end. This is the beginning."

He only nodded as he pulled his arm out of the cell, stepped back, and fiddled awkwardly with his Band until it was free from his wrist.

"Take this. For luck." He held it out to me.

I pushed his hand away, shaking my head.

"No. I can't take your father's Band. This should be in your family."

He thrust it back with a little more force.

"Take it. Don't be stubborn about everything all the time. I want you to have it. You can use it when you start crawling again. The best Crawler with the most powerful Band in all of the Lowlands."

He smiled, and my breath got caught in my chest when I saw the deep affection in his eyes. I conceded with a nod and took the Band.

"Thank you," I said, lowering my gaze to my feet. "I'll return it someday. I'm not sure I'll ever be crawling again, but I promise I'll return it when I'm free, and all of this is over."

He slid his hand through the cage again and lifted my chin until his eyes held mine.

"My mother once told me that life is a risk. I didn't know what she meant until I loved you."

I swayed and choked down the burning in the back of my throat. I wanted to hear the beat of his heart against my ear.

"Then you'll understand why I'm doing what I'm doing. I can't live like this anymore. *We* can't live like this anymore."

"Visiting time is over."

The guard had reappeared, and I honestly didn't care how much of our conversation he had overheard. It wouldn't matter anyway.

Asher nodded and brushed his thumb along my jawline. "I don't want a life without you in it."

His hand fell away as the guard ushered him down the hall-way. I watched Asher walk away, feeling even more alone than I had before he arrived.

44

I couldn't sleep. Not like I would have expected to in a roach-filled prison cell while waiting for the Chief to decide whether he was going to turn me over to Corvus.

It had felt so good to see Asher, to feel his touch. But with that comfort had come a new set of feelings that I couldn't quite process. Although I hadn't been able to articulate my feelings for my friend while he'd been standing in front of me, I had realized something else—he represented the weak, subservient class that I couldn't be a part of any longer. Asher wasn't a fool, and he wasn't a pacifist, but he had been conditioned to conform; raised to believe that the Crows were superior to Hydrans and that we should simply bow to Corvus and do what we're told.

History is never made by people who just do what they're told.

The sound of the outer door's rusty hinges preceded the footfalls coming down the steps. I didn't bother to stand up or look down the hallway. The only person I cared about had already come to my cell, and I doubted that Sandor would let Asher return to see me again so soon.

"Stubbornness runs in your family."

I thought he was making a joke, as he smiled at me from the other side of my cell. I swung my legs from the cot and looked at him, not saying a word.

"I've been discussing this *situation* with my advisors. Things with Corvus are not good."

"You think? He's already burned our crops."

Sandor held up his hands. "We want to help you. Protect you. But you've got to help yourself first."

"I don't know what that means."

He smiled again and cocked his head to the side.

"I am a fair and just leader. My decisions are always made in the best interest of our village. I have always had the greatest respect for your family. I knew your grandfather well. He was a good man. I respected your father, although I didn't agree with his ideologies and I certainly didn't support the revolution." He paused and brushed his fingertips against the steel cage. "Don't end up like your father, fighting for something you can't possibly win."

"We can't win anything without a fight."

He rubbed his fingertips together. Flakes of brown rust floated to the floor. "Now you even sound like him."

I paused, feeling as though Sandor had come here expecting me to be contrite so that he could go back to Corvus and tell the man that everything was under control, that there would be no further complications.

But there would be further complications.

"Nice Band."

I looked down and realized I'd been spinning Asher's Band around my wrist, my fingers feeling for the unseen forces in the most powerful magnetic Band ever used in the Lowlands.

"It was a gift. Passed down to Asher from his father. But I guess our aluminum trade is kind of pointless now."

At the time, I didn't understand why Sandor laughed when I

said that, but I'd later realize that we weren't talking about the Band at all.

"You can be legendary, Rayna. A Crawler for the ages. You're already the best, and now you have that."

Was Sandor in denial?

"Crawling for Corvus? So the Crows can pointlessly hoard the aluminum and hand us rat-infested grain? Yes, the stuff of legends."

"Do you realize I'm trying to keep you from hanging? Corvus wants the person responsible for the breach of the Nest executed. I believe I have a way to appease him that would spare your life. But you must stop this nonsense right now and do what I say. Can you do that?"

45

I awoke with a start, gravel stinging my eyelids as I opened them. I sat upright in the prison cot, shaking my head and spitting, dirt on my lips and in my mouth.

"Wake up."

The nasal tone of Jaef's voice filled my ears. I scowled as I realized he had kicked dirt at my cot. I stood up, clenched my fists, and faced him.

"What do you want?"

His eyes shimmered like green icicles, his thin lips woven tight. "I've come to talk to you, and you're going to listen."

"I have no interest in what you have to say."

I swung my eyes from him and looked at the barred window. Pink light at the horizon illuminated the early morning sky.

"Well, you're gonna listen anyway."

I squared my chin and focused on the window. I wouldn't give him the satisfaction of my undivided attention, despite the fact that he was right. I had no choice but to listen.

"This isn't just about you. We're paying for your actions—the entire Hydran village. We're being punished for what you did, and it's not fair. At all."

When I didn't respond, he continued.

"What would your grandfather say? Would he approve of your disobedience?"

I watched clouds drifting through the brilliant colors of the burgeoning sunrise, high and thin.

"Rayna!"

I jerked at the sound of his voice. Why wouldn't he just go away? I whirled around to look at him, my face glowering red.

"What?"

"Answer me."

I walked to the edge of the cell where I'd stood talking to Asher the night before. I could smell the lake on Jaef—dead fish and rust—and it made me want to vomit.

"What's done is done. I can't undo it."

"But you can make it right. Obey the rules and follow the laws or more people will get hurt. Or is that what you want?"

I shook my head. Of course I didn't want anyone else to get hurt, but this moron had yet to accept what was at stake, what sort of life he was asking me to preserve. I might have been in the village prison, but Corvus had kept the village in a special sort of prison for generations, and most of us hadn't even realized we were inmates.

"Corvus is leaning hard on Sandor. He wants someone to be held accountable for this mess, but the Chief can be persuasive. This only works if you're willing to do what Sandor says. You have to take responsibility for your actions, or we're all gonna suffer. You need to do what Sandor says—do you hear me?"

"I'm standing right in front you, aren't I?"

His brows raised and what appeared to be a glimmer of hope flashed across Jaef's face. He seemed to be in denial as well, as if I was the only one willing to face the brutal truth of what the Crows had been making us do for decades.

"Then you'll do the right thing. Save our village."

It was a statement rather than a question, but I felt compelled to answer. Honestly.

"I will do the right thing for us all. I will save our village."

---

a gust of wind blew through my cell window and made
me shiver. I sat cross-legged on the cot, my eyes closed
as streaks of sun filtered through the bars and provided a bit of
warmth. I took deliberate breaths, trying to convince myself that
the path I'd chosen was the right one. Although he'd been a
lunkheaded jerk, Jaef was right. What I did in the next several
days would have consequences for not just me, but the entire
village and maybe beyond. I would have much preferred to be
alone and back in my old life, crawling the bottom of the lake.
But I had to face the truth of the moment and realize that
people's lives depended on my actions.

I heard a man clear his throat. I opened my eyes and turned to
face the front of the cell.

"Chief Sandor."

He gave me a curt nod and a grave stare.

"Rayna. I trust you've had enough time to consider my
proposal?"

I stood up and walked over so that I faced our village leader
with nothing but rusty bars between us.

"I have."

His lips stretched into a forced smile. "Good. I knew you were smart enough to understand how explosive things are right now. Our relations with Corvus haven't been this strained since..."

He trailed off, and I knew why. He didn't want to bring up my father's insurgency again.

"I understand. You're right. Things now are bad between the Crows and us."

Sandor nodded, a long sigh escaping his lips. "Good, good. You had me worried."

I went to the words I'd rehearsed in my head dozens of times before I lost my nerve.

"I've scoured the depths of Lake Union, just like my parents and grandparents before me, and for a good reason. To find aluminum for the Crows which we trade so they can provide the machines for our fields and rations that keep us alive. Without the fertilizer and livestock they supply, we wouldn't eat. We'd have to venture into the dangerous forests, sort of like the problem we have now."

He nodded again, and I could see the tension melting from his shoulders. I stepped back and began to walk in a slow circle around my cell.

I continued. "I know Corvus hasn't treated us fairly and that he's made things really hard on you. But without the protection from the Crows, we'd be in trouble. Between the farms and their arms, we owe them a lot."

His lips now stretched wide. "I knew you were smart and would understand my predicament. I have a plan in place that I believe will satisfy Corvus. Now, you might have to do more time in this—"

"I'm not finished."

I stopped my loop and stood beneath the window, staring out into the blue sky as I spoke.

"But now I know the truth. I know that all our sacrifices mean nothing, that the heaps of aluminum hoarded by the metal merchants are pointless. They've done nothing but draw rats for decades. The Crows living in the Nest don't live like us. Even the Corvax live better than us, and they're outcasts on Queen Anne Hill."

"But Rayna—"

"They eat bacon," I said, now turning to see that Sandor's mouth had fallen open and his face turned bright red.

"I have a meeting with Corvus in an hour."

"Then I guess you'd better start thinking about what you're going to tell him. I will not admit to anything. And, I'm done following the unjust and unfair laws that have been used on us for generations. I won't let my friends and family die in vain, and I will not serve Corvus anymore. I'm done."

Sandor's face went from red to white, and he stepped back from the bars. "What are you saying?"

"I can't do it. I can't be the sacrificial lamb you put in front of Corvus. I can't keep risking my life crawling for worthless metal. I can't put my tail between my legs and bow to the monster who took my friend's hand, executed a kid in front of our village and murdered my parents. I won't obey any longer."

He closed his eyes, and his wide chest heaved under the thick robe. I lifted my chin high and stared at him, unblinking.

He opened his eyes and shook his head while lowering the volume of his booming voice to barely a whisper. "You will not confess to Corvus?"

"I will not."

"Then God have mercy on our souls."

I watched him walk away and out of sight, presumably on his way to grovel before Lord Corvus. I didn't care whether he told him I was responsible or not. He was the Chief. Let him deal with the political fallout.

My conscience had been cleared, and I felt a weight come off my shoulders as if I'd just broken the surface of the water after a long crawl. I might have been in a prison cell, but for the first time in my life, I believed I was truly free.

What I didn't realize was that saying so didn't mean it was true. Freedom is fought for and earned, never given.

he sound of the screams pierced my ears, and I knew I'd never forget those forsaken cries of my people. Time slowed to a creep as I scrambled to the window, using the edge of the cot to haul myself up to get a better view. I could see one intersection of two roads running perpendicular to the village. The thoroughfare before me had huts on three corners and a marketplace on the fourth. It stood empty, which in and of itself was not normal. When I saw the flames engulf the hut and a woman running with her children in tow, however, I knew my worst fears had come true.

In an instant, villagers flooded the streets. I watched help-lessly from the windows as arrows sliced the air from all direc-tions, finding their marks and spearing the backs of Hydran men, women, and children as they cried out.

Crow soldiers galloped in on horseback carrying swords, clubs, and burning torches. They wore studded leather for armor, their lower faces concealed with dirty bandanas, and they rode through the streets killing any Hydrans within reach. The heavy, thick, black smoke began to cloud out the sun, and the sickly-sweet smell of burning flesh filled my nostrils.

My head began to throb and I doubled over, gagging and trying not to vomit. What was happening? It would have been impossible for Sandor to get to Corvus and talk to him so quickly after the Chief had left my cell. I jumped from the cot and peered through a crack in the opposite wall and into the village.

Blood orange flames licked rooftops, relentless in their incinerating consumption as they charred every hut in sight. More black smoke marred the air like devastating ink. I saw people running and falling, some bowing to the Crow soldiers only to be slaughtered like sheep. Some villagers scampered toward the woods, others to the lake.

Despite witnessing such heinous acts, I did my best to focus and think rationally. The only explanation was that Corvus had lost patience, ordering the attack even before speaking to Sandor. It was the only thing that made sense. That wretched, evil man had probably never been made to wait in his life, sitting like a king in his Needle above the filth of the Lowlands.

I heard a thump and then crackling. The prison had been set on fire.

I whirled around and grabbed at the gates, rattling the rusted bars as hard as I could, figuring that if I shook them hard enough, I might be able to break out.

The rust came off the bars in clouds of orange dust as I shook them, but they wouldn't budge. I was about to scream out the window when the prison doors at the top of the staircase swung open, and a flood of light drenched the hallway leading to my cell. I listened, but heard no other cries from inside the prison, meaning I was the only inmate inside—a fact most Hydrans and Crows probably knew.

A bulky figure cast a long shadow down the stairwell. I craned my neck for a better view. Perhaps Sandor had sent someone to let me out, thinking I would give myself up and end the madness.

"Hey!" I called, pressing my face against the cold steel. "Hey! Let me out!"

A Crow soldier came down the hallway, and I saw the arrow-head first, pointed right at me. I shrunk back from the bars, having no weapon and nowhere to hide.

The soldier stopped in front of my cell, a wide grin spreading across his face. "The rebel. Right where you're supposed to be."

"Take me to Corvus. I need to speak to him."

"He's done talking, love. I'm here to make sure we don't ever have to deal with this problem again."

He pulled back the drawstring of his bow. I stood tall, my chin out and my eyes locked on his. I wouldn't die cowering, nor would I beg for my life from a thug who wouldn't listen to me anyway.

The soldier sneered at me, and then his face twisted. Blood trickled from the corner of his mouth. As I looked down, I could see the tip of a spear protruding from the soldier's throat. He stood for another moment before collapsing to the ground, revealing another figure who had been standing behind the soldier in the hallway.

Asher.

48

"Hold on."

He fumbled with an old, rusted set of keys until he found the one that unlocked my cell. I looked at the man on the ground, blood pooling around his body. Asher had taken a life to save mine, and I couldn't catch my breath. I had been standing there, expecting death from the soldier's bow, but my friend had come back for me.

A sharp, piercing sound cut through the sounds of battle coming through my window as the rusty hinges gave way. I grabbed the bars and pulled the gate toward me before stepping around them and into Asher's arms. I huddled forward and pressed my ear to his chest, listening to the flutter of his heart for a fleeting second.

His arm came around me.

"Are you okay?"

I could only nod as I choked back the tears threatening to spill out. A loud crack came from above us as the prison roof began to cave under the flames. I tore myself away from him.

"There's no time!"

The raging fire was eating away at the ancient timbers

supporting the roof of the prison, and I could feel the heat radiating off the concrete blocks. Thick, black smoke poured into the building, and I began coughing uncontrollably. I pulled my shirt up over my mouth. Asher handed the soldier's bow and quiver to me, and then pulled the spear from the body of the dead man.

"Ready?"

I could taste the bitter smoke on my lips, and felt it burning in my lungs.

"Yes."

Asher ran down the hallway, and I followed. I couldn't remember being brought into the prison, and the smoke made it almost impossible to see. I reached out as we moved, checking to see that each cell was open and that nobody had been left to burn alive inside them.

"Empty," said Asher as he turned to hurry me along. "You were the only one left in here."

I looked up the staircase to where the door opened out upon a world of chaos. The daylight filled the frame above the billowing smoke as if the threshold hung in the high clouds of a storm. I guessed, in a way, it did. I knew that once I marched out of the burning prison I would be stepping into a new realm. Things in my village had changed. Forever.

"Hurry!"

Asher nudged me with the butt end of his spear. I hadn't realized I'd stopped, caught in my own thoughts in the midst of the fire. I followed him up the staircase, my bow in one hand and an arrow in the other. The tip of Asher's spear led the way.

When I crossed the threshold and ran from the intense fire that had engulfed the prison, I stumbled to the ground in a fit of coughs that wouldn't stop. Asher had fallen next to me, on his knees and struggling to get fresh air into his scalded lungs.

I rolled over onto my back once I was able to catch my breath, wiping the black soot from my face. I opened my eyes to see the brilliant blue sky above while the sounds of death rained down upon me.

I sat up and looked around.

Bodies everywhere. Crow soldiers raced through the streets, shooting or stabbing any Hydran they'd come across. I saw children and mothers lying motionless in every direction I looked. Some of the kids I'd crawled with—my friends—were fighting Corvus' men, some with clubs and others with their bare fists. I shook my head and wiped at my eyes, uncertain if what I was seeing was really happening. The smoke from the fires had cast a heavy blanket on the village, and now it seemed as though all of the violence was happening in a hazy, dreamlike state. But this was no dream, and it was no nightmare. The reality was far worse.

"That way. The avenue will take us to the edge of the forest."

Asher was still coughing, but he'd managed to get enough fresh air into his lungs to speak.

"What?" It felt as though the hot ash had filled my chest like I was drowning in fire.

"They won't chase us there. We can hide and be safe until this is all over."

I looked around again as men continued to fight, and bleed, and die. I saw a child running down the street, shoeless and shirtless while screaming for his mother.

"No."

"No what, Rayna?"

"I'm not hiding. I'm not running. Not while they're killing our people."

"But there's so many of them. And they have better weap—"

"Then go. Hide. I'm staying, and I'm fighting. I'd rather die free than live imprisoned. They've had us in chains, Asher. And I'm done with that."

A cry interrupted Asher's response. I whirled around as a Crow soldier on horseback charged at me, an iron club swinging in his hand. I ducked and turned to fire my arrow, which hit the man, knocking him off the horse. He was dead before he hit the ground.

In one motion, I had another arrow from the quiver nocked and aimed at a second soldier on horseback riding right for us. I fired and missed. His eyes lit up and he pushed the horse harder, quickly closing the distance as he raised his spear. Asher stepped in front of me, but I knocked him aside. I fired a second arrow at the attacker, and this one also hit the mark—a bullseye in the middle of his forehead.

All of those hours of secret weapons practice at the Troll had paid off in a way I could have never anticipated.

"How many?"

Asher's mouth hung open as he looked at the two men I'd shot and then back to me. I grabbed him by the shoulders and shook him.

"How many Crow soldiers are here?"

"Twenty? Thirty? I don't really know. As soon as I saw that they'd set the prison on fire, I came for you."

I looked around. The smoke had intensified, and now I was barely able to see anything except amorphous shapes moving through the haze like revenants. But a gust of wind came off the lake and pushed the curtain of smoke aside to reveal what awaited us behind it.

Ten Crow soldiers had seen us, about 100 yards away and approaching with spears raised.

49

I had pieced it together almost instantly, my thoughts galvanized by the threat of the Crow soldiers marching toward us. Sandor had been hoping to negotiate with Corvus, who'd expected the Chief to deliver the guilty party to him. Our fields had already been burned, the stern message sent to the Hydrans. But here I stood in the middle of the destruction, an insignificant village in the Lowlands burned to the ground by Corvus. And he'd commanded his soldiers to find me and kill me. That left only one explanation—Corvus had discovered that it was me who had met with Shepherd and gone into the Nest, and he'd lost patience with the situation. He must have believed that crushing this rebellion now and obliterating the village would prevent others from doing the same. Corvus wanted to make an example out of our village, and he'd called for my head.

"That's her. That's the one Lord Corvus wants dead."

"She's innocent. She's done nothing."

A soldier ran over and smacked Asher in the mouth, knocking him to the ground and dislodging the spear from his hand.

"Shut up, stump."

The soot mixed with sweat bit at my eyes like tiny needles and

191

the man who had hit Asher turned to face me, thinking that I'd begun to cry. He held up his hand to the soldiers who had tightened the circle around us. They stopped, obeying the unspoken command of their superior.

"What's wrong, honey? Don't like what happens when you break the law?"

I sniffled, and that seemed to thrill him even more. He looked over his shoulder at one of the other Crow soldiers, a gap-toothed smile forming on his ashy face.

"Aw. She's gonna cry. C'mon, girl. Cry for us before we bring your head back to our Lord on a spike."

Asher climbed to his feet and staggered backward, trying to keep his balance. He shook his head and pinched the top of his nose with his thumb and forefinger. He blinked and looked at me. I winked.

"Please, sir. This is all a misunderstanding. I requested to speak to Corvus from my cell. I'll obey. I promise."

I looked past the soldiers, seeing the bodies piled up in the village as Corvus' men continued to rout the untrained poor, farmers and Crawlers alike. Although pockets of fighting remained, the cries of pain and suffering seemed to be getting swallowed by the dead.

"Nah. Too late. The Lord said bring back yer head. That's what we aim to do."

The spear whistled through the air so quickly that, at first, I wasn't sure what it was. The soldier who had been standing in front of me dropped to his knees with his hands on his throat. A spear had gone through his neck, the tip extending two feet out the other side. Blood shot from the severed artery, arching into the air in time with the man's fading heartbeat. Three more soldiers fell then, each one now in the dirt and trying to dislodge the spears that had penetrated their bodies.

I looked at Asher and saw that he was looking at the second floor of a hut that, for some reason, had not yet burned to the ground. I saw silhouettes standing in the broken windows and recognized them even without seeing their faces—Jaef's goons.

"What the—"

Before Asher could finish asking the question, one of the soldiers grabbed his club. He yanked me by the arm and used me as a human shield in the hopes that whoever had ambushed them wouldn't risk hitting me. The other soldiers turned and ran hard for the building where the snipers had hidden.

"I'm not dying in this godforsaken pit. I'll drag you all the way to the Needle if I have to and let Corvus do what he pleases with you."

Asher bent down for his spear.

"And unless you want to lose your other hand, drop it."

I thought we were finished. I was certain Asher would die defending me, and then the Crow soldiers would tie me up and take me to Corvus.

"Good! You found her."

That high-pitched, shrill voice. I would have recognized it anywhere.

"Who are you?" the soldier holding me asked Jaef, who stood next to him with a long dagger. "And what are you doing?"

"Sandor sent me to make sure she didn't escape."

"Well, Corvus called for her head, so buzz off before we take you, too."

Jaef cackled and grabbed me by the hair.

"That's fine. As long as this one gets what's coming to her."

The soldier smiled, his eyes moving from my feet to my chest. Lingering on my chest.

I noticed that Jaef had glanced over his shoulder twice at the building where his goons had been stationed. The Crow soldiers had headed toward the building to kill them. That meant that the only Crow soldier within eyesight of us was the creep clutching my arm.

"One more thing," Jaef said to the soldier.

"Yeah? What's that?"

"Don't forget your knife."

Jaef lunged forward, burying his dagger in the man's chest and then twisting it. The soldier let go of my arm and dropped to his knees, blood pouring from his open mouth. Asher looked up, his face as pale as the harvest moon. Jaef put his boot on the man's shoulder, yanked the dagger free, and kicked him into the dirt before turning a sneer on me.

"Don't think that makes us friends, *rebel*."

Before I could respond, Jaef ran toward the building where his friends had lured the soldiers inside, presumably to pick them off one at a time.

My head swirled with a thousand questions. What was Jaef doing? Why was he killing Crow soldiers? And, at the same time, why had he saved my life? It was Asher who brought my attention back to the seriousness of the situation.

"Rayna, come on. Jaef gave us a chance. We have to get out of here before the soldiers come back or Corvus sends more."

He was right. Every second I stood there contemplating the surreal events of the last twelve hours—hell, of the last twelve minutes—was increasing the risk of us being killed or captured. The time to fight would come again, and I would rush into it headlong. But not now. We had to get out of the village and hide until the immediate danger had passed. It pained me to think about all the people we had to leave behind, including Ember. But Corvus was after me and maybe I could draw his soldiers out of the village if I fled. We couldn't stand up to his entire army and the two of us couldn't save everyone in that moment.

"You're right," I said. "I know of some hunting grounds on the western edge of the forest. Follow me."

Asher bent down and picked up his spear, following me as I ran from the fire and blood that had consumed the village.

y head rattled as I left behind the chaotic sounds of war, bolting as fast as I could toward the outskirts of the village. I heard Asher's quick, raspy breaths close behind me. The stretch of the green canopy loomed ahead like a dark, mysterious haven. My boots pounded the muddy ground, my legs feeling wobbly. I was almost to the forest, where we would hide within the tall trees and thick vines.

I hadn't thought much about the decision. Normally, running straight into the dark unknown was not something I'd willingly do. But we didn't have a choice. We'd be killed by Crow soldiers, or we'd be attacked by the monsters of the woods.

The closer we got, though, the more I felt the resistance rising inside of me. Since we'd been children, Hydran elders warned us of the mad, feral creatures living in the wilderness. We crawled the lake for more than just the aluminum quotas set by Corvus and delivered to the Nest. Deep down, we all knew that exploring the submerged, dark recesses of Union meant we didn't have to enter the dangerous corners of the wooded Lowlands, those beyond the worn paths between the village and the forgotten ruins.

I ignored the shouts of the Crow soldiers, keeping my eyes on the tree line and praying we hadn't been followed. Two more strides and I'd be there.

Lunging forward, I slipped past two oaks and squirmed through a wall of ivy, realizing too late that it may have been Leaves of Three I'd passed, which would almost certainly give me a rash. But I'd made it out of the village. I turned to look back at Asher and stopped short. He was twenty yards behind me, stumbling toward the tree line, still with his hand on his stomach. I hadn't seen it, but it looked like he'd been injured in the fighting.

"C'mon!" I yelled with a forced whisper, trying to encourage him to run while at the same time not giving up my position to the Crow soldiers pursuing us. I waved my arms frantically as I watched him from behind the ivy. "Hurry up!"

Asher's face had turned blue, his chest heaving. I'd forgotten that his weak lungs would have slowed him down under normal circumstances, and this was nothing even close to normal.

A shimmer moved across his blue eyes as they locked on mine. I smiled, my face still partially hidden in the dark, green leaves. I gave him an encouraging nod, as he had closed the gap and was now only fifteen feet from the tree line.

When Asher stopped, and his mouth opened soundlessly, I clasped my hands to my mouth. An arrowhead had appeared through Asher's left shoulder, then another just over his right hip. He dropped to his knees, revealing two Crow archers behind him.

"No!"

This time, I couldn't mask the volume of my voice, and I saw the soldiers lift their heads and start to run toward the tree line. When I looked back at Asher, he'd already collapsed to the ground and wasn't moving.

A whistle sounded, and more Crow soldiers raced toward us. I wasn't sure if they'd run into the forest. I wondered if Crow parents told their children the same horror stories about the wilderness.

"She's in there," I heard one of them say, but none of the soldiers came toward me, as if each one was waiting to use someone else's courage.

I was alone, my village turned into ash. The last thing I wanted to do was to run *deeper* into the forest, but my only other option was to surrender. That wasn't about to happen.

"Get her!"

Whatever reluctance the Crow soldiers had felt about entering the forest had evaporated, and now they all came after me. I took another look at Asher's body on the ground as the Crow soldiers closed in, their bows raised and bloody swords in hand.

I turned around, and pushed through the ivy and into the darkened woods that blocked out most of the late-morning daylight. There was nothing I could do for Asher, and standing still would most likely result in my being captured or killed.

I ran as fast as I could, dodging tree trunks and my own tears as I muttered his name repeatedly. The black void of the cursed forest had seeped into my heart, as well.

51

J couldn't be sure exactly how long I'd been running. The concept of time eluded me, yet my feet kept moving me deeper into the forest. It was only when the last rays of the sun had filtered through the treetops and evaporated into a dirty, dusk sky that my legs gave out and I collapsed.

The Crow soldiers had come for me. Fighting back the same instinctive revulsion I'd had for the forest, they'd chased me through the trees before eventually giving up and turning back sometime before nightfall. I didn't know it for sure, but I'd neither seen nor heard any sign of them since about midday.

Without the constant threat of an arrow going through my chest, my head began to catch up with my feet. I thought about my grandfather, my friends, crawling, Asher. The memories and feelings swirled inside of me as I focused on the last glimpse I'd had of my village—a burning, black husk that had been destroyed in mere moments by Corvus; the bitter taste of ash was still souring my mouth, the dying cries of villagers filling my ears. In my mind, I saw Asher's body on the ground, and I couldn't hold it together, the sobs were suddenly coming up from deep inside. He'd sacrificed himself for me so that I could escape.

My body shook as if the ground beneath me had turned into an angry lake. I was utterly alone, the frustration and hopelessness escaping in a sudden scream that tore from my vocal chords and silenced the strange birds in the trees.

Night stalked me, and I could feel the temperature rapidly falling. I needed to find somewhere to rest and stay warm while not being discovered, should Corvus have sent his men after me. I was so thirsty that I chewed on several large leaves, trying to extract as much moisture as I could from them. Grasping each trunk as I passed, I continued deeper into the forest and farther from what remained of my old life.

With the sun completely down, I'd catch a glimpse of the stars through the thick blanket of leaves above. Their flickering light was sprinkled across the black sky like lucid lanterns and, somehow, they encouraged me to keep going. Just as I rounded a thick trunk, I heard a noise that didn't sound like an animal. I stopped and listened, trying to silence the blood rushing in my ears.

People. They were talking. I couldn't tell where they were or who they were, though, so I took slow, deliberate steps and avoided the brittle branches on the forest floor. In a crevice between two massive boulders, I found three shapes huddled together at the mouth of a narrow cave. They saw me at the same time as I saw them, jumping like startled rabbits.

"It's okay." I showed them my palms as I approached the cave.

They looked at me with wide eyes, merely children.

The biggest kid in the group snapped at me. "We know who you are. You started all this. Get away from us!"

"I'm not going to hurt you. Promise."

The oldest of the three boys had bright red hair and blue eyes, his frame wiry and lean. I remembered seeing him around the village, but he wasn't a Crawler and not a regular at the Troll because I think he was a year or two younger than me—maybe sixteen or seventeen.

The other two children made me pause and shake my head.

They each wore the same type of buttoned shirt, seemingly with ash staining the fabric in the exact same places. I noted how dark-haired they were, and with their piercing green eyes, I could imagine these two boys becoming handsome men. And then I realized the reason they'd been wearing the same clothes.

Twins. Identical.

"We don't have a village thanks to her. Everyone is dead."

"And you will be, too, if you don't lower your voice. We don't know if the soldiers are still following us."

They fell silent and looked around in the dark, the whites of their eyes hovering on faces covered in soot. The oldest kid stepped toward me, lowering his voice.

"Have you seen them?"

"No. But that doesn't mean they're not coming. I can help you, but you have to help me. We're all Hydrans, right?"

I couldn't see their expressions in the dark, but nobody said a word.

"Listen. I'm tired. I need some water and some rest. Can you help me or not?"

"Not!"

I huffed and turned in the direction of the twins, one of whom had snapped at me. "Fine. Good luck when the creatures come out for their night hunt..."

I'd started to walk away when the older boy grabbed my arm.

"Wait."

One twin pushed a canteen at me, his lips tight and his eyes brimming with hate.

"Here, but just a sip. It's all we got."

I took a swig and handed the canteen back.

"Thank you. Now, may I sit and rest my legs?"

Nobody protested, so I sat down and put my back against the cold rock, staring up at the stars and wishing I could be in the sky, high above all this madness.

"So, what are your names?"

The elder boy spoke first. "I'm Baylock. These are my brothers, Alaric and Thisbe."

"I'm Rayna." I smiled, but I knew they couldn't see it through the inky veil between us.

"They say you're to blame for this. That Corvus killed everyone because he was looking for you."

"Do you think it's my fault that a madman destroyed our village because he was looking for me?"

Baylock sighed, and I could almost see him nod. "Our parents. Our sister. Probably all…"

"Yeah, probably." I swallowed hard. "We've all lost a lot."

"When can we go back?" The twins spoke, almost as one voice. "Yeah, I wanna go home. Do you think we can?"

Alaric and Thisbe didn't understand what was happening. And, how could they? I looked closer while my eyes adjusted to the darkness, realizing that they were far younger than I'd thought, maybe nine or ten.

"Listen, our homes have been destroyed by the Crows, our people have been slaughtered like pigs. We can't go back to how it was. Nothing will ever be the same again." I leaned in closer to the boys. "It's time to fight for our freedom."

They were silent as they considered my words. Then Baylock spoke.

"How? There's only my two kid brothers and us."

"I don't know. Right now, I'm more concerned with staying alive and finding others who escaped from our village. But every set of hands will help. Even young ones."

He looked down at his twin brothers, ruffling each kid's hair with a different hand. They looked up at their older brother with shallow grins, and it almost broke my heart. I had a feeling there would be more tragedy before Hydran children would be able to smile again.

Baylock nodded. "For now, these little guys need to get some sleep. Who knows what tomorrow will bring?"

I decided not to say anything else, especially about being in the forest. At night. Having the boys there gave me a bit of comfort, but the old monster stories of our youth would intensify as the moon rose.

My adrenaline had worn off, and even though I was cold and hungry, I had a hard time keeping my eyes open, so I curled up against a tree trunk and fell into a restless sleep until the dawn light woke me.

The birds twittered above as I rubbed my sleepy eyes and blinked at the brothers, their pale faces smeared with ash and dirt. The twins played with sticks in the dirt while Baylock stared at me. When I looked at him directly, he quickly turned away.

"What?" I pulled myself up, my muscles stiff and my neck tight.

Baylock scrunched up his nose and shrugged. "It's just that..."

"He thinks you're pretty," said Thisbe.

At least I thought it was Thisbe.

"You *like* her." Alaric chimed in with an emphasis on the second word.

"No. Shut up. Both of you. I mean, 'no' I don't like you, not 'no' you're not pretty. I mean..."

I waved my hand at them all and decided to let Baylock off the hook while his younger brothers continued to giggle at his expense.

"After Sandor threw you in jail, everyone in the village said you were guilty. Nothing but trouble. I didn't want to go anywhere near you."

I raised my eyebrows and sighed. "They were right. I am trouble."

That made Baylock smile. He stood up and brushed the dirt from his pants.

"Now what? Where do we go?"

The previous night had been all about survival, and I honestly hadn't thought this far ahead. Maybe subconsciously I'd believed the old tales of the forest creatures abducting children in the night, not expecting us to even be there in the morning.

"We should double-back toward the village. I'm sure the Crows have returned to the Nest, and it would give us a chance to find other survivors. We can't be the only ones to have escaped."

"Okay. Then maybe we can figure out how we're going to fight back."

"See?" I put my hands on my hips as I stood. "My rebellious ways are rubbing off on you."

Baylock helped the twins up, and we gathered the few items we'd had in our possession before turning east toward the village. I could still smell the burning wood in the air, and the ash continued to fall like a light mist.

I took two steps from our hiding place and found myself on the edge of a clearing, a rectangular-shaped field bordered on all sides.

Something struck the side of my head. I staggered, falling into Baylock. Blood trickled from a cut on my temple as all the brothers froze, staring at the group of people who had surrounded us.

I couldn't remember ever seeing this tribe before. The visitors wore khaki-style tops with thick belts and fingerless gloves, their boots stretching to their knees. They smelled like soured cheese and rotting fish.

"Who are you?"

Nobody answered my question. The twin brothers cowered behind my back while Baylock stood next to me. I could sense the strength in the guy as he tried to protect his brothers and me from these invaders.

"Shut up, *Crawler*."

An older man, apparently the leader of the gang, stepped forward and began to tie my wrists together. Other men did the same to Baylock and the twins.

A younger man, not much older than me, stepped around the older guy and used his filthy fingers to lift my chin. He smiled, missing all of his front teeth and smelling as though he hadn't swum in a lake in months. I almost gagged when he leaned in and spoke to the others.

"She'll fetch a high bid. And the little ones will, too. Probably should put him down. Ain't worth our rations to keep him alive."

My hands clenched into fists, and Baylock stepped forward even while they were binding his wrists. "You won't touch her. Or them."

The man chuckled and opened his arms, turning to face the others. "Don't touch them. They're special."

The others laughed as dozens more came through the trees and into the clearing. All those old stories had turned out to be true.

There were monsters in the forest. And we had become their captives.

CONTINUE READING THE CRAWLING GIRL BOOK TWO

BATTLE CROW CHAPTER 1

*T*he only real cell is the one between our ears but I was too young back then to figure it out.

The days passed in a smoldering blur of blinding afternoon sun and frigid nights with the odor of human feces. The prisoners' sweat smelled like desperation, impossible to ignore and laced with hopelessness. I hadn't inhaled the forest air for days, and although the high desert provided some relief from the humidity, it punished us with ungodly heat.

I felt my heart racing, my eyes buzzing in their sockets. The bars of my cage had rubbed the skin raw on my lower back.

I'd grown accustomed to the sounds of horseshoes clipping against the compacted desert sand, a thin layer of silicon covering the old asphalt trails. The constant rattling of the caged bars had become a soothing friend, something to distract me from my thoughts. My focus kept coming back to memories of Asher, helplessly watching him collapse to the ground in a flurry of arrows fired by Crow soldiers.

I pulled my legs tight against my chest, clasping my fingers over my knees to hold them steady as I tried not to lean back against the rusty bars. Whoever these criminals were, they had put all of us Hydrans in a locked cart pulled by horses—an animal's cage on wheels. One of the kids they'd captured looked at me, his blistered lips opening and his wide-set brown eyes sunken but staring into mine.

"I can't. I just can't."

He leaned his head back against the iron bars, proceeding to knock his head against them repeatedly. Rust flaked onto his shoulders and a trickle of blood mixed with the sweat rolling down his neck.

"Shut up." Even whispering those two words broke open the sores on the inside of my mouth. "You can, and you will."

I had become a prisoner, like the others in the cart. The filthy men who captured me had pushed me into the rusty cage like herded cattle, cracking whips, cursing, and spitting tobacco in our faces. Baylock and the twins had been ushered onto another cart before setting off in the opposite direction. That was the last I'd seen of them.

An endless blue spread from one barren horizon to the other. I hadn't seen water—in a bottle or in a lake—in days and I felt as though my soul had shriveled. In my entire life, I'd never spent so much time away from it. We'd traveled east, that much I knew based on the motion of the sun. From what I could remember of my grandfather's stories, we had to have been in the high desert, in a land once known as Nevada. Far from home.

Home. The thought made my stomach churn with curdled hate. Corvus had destroyed our village, killed my friends, and then burnt it to the ground before sending his soldiers after us. If I hadn't been so deep in the forest running from the Crows, I wouldn't have been in this situation. I hated Corvus, Sandor, and all the responsible adults of the village who were supposed to protect us. I knew I'd eventually escape, and when I did, I'd be free to go anywhere. But that wasn't the plan. I could taste revenge on my lips.

You could say hate was love moving in the wrong direction. I would destroy the Crows and set things right, making sure everyone had an equal chance at a good life. Or I would die trying.

The desert air had been extremely dry but also dusty. The dirt billowed out from the wagon wheels on the cart and I tried to suppress a cough so as to not catch the attention of the guards who had beaten other prisoners for less. But my lungs were weak, and before I knew it, I was barking with an uncontrollable fit of dry coughs.

"Ay. What's going on back there?"

I froze and dropped my eyes as the wagon slowed to a halt.

Through snippets of conversation I'd snuck with other prisoners, and by listening to our captors as they talked, I'd figured out that they sold people for resources. They sold slaves. While the Crows had imprisoned us in meaningless ritual, these men used cages.

My eyes darted toward the men on horseback who rode ahead, their eyes hardened and their skin leathered with beards to protect their faces from the brutal sun. They had circled back around when the wagon slowed, escorted by several dogs with bald patches, sores, and yellow teeth. The beasts yelped and whined as the men snapped whips on their behinds.

The men on horseback stopped next to the guards on the reins of our cage, their restless horses sending another cloud of dust into the air. I couldn't hear the voices of our captors; their exchange had been too low and hoarse to understand.

"...dump the dead ones. But let's hope we don't lose any of our cargo."

That was all I could hear, but it was enough to tell me how much our lives meant to the slavers. Not much.

One of the men riding on the cart looked at me with dark, beady eyes as the men riding the horses trotted alongside of it. My heart began to thump a little harder as one of them cocked his mammoth-like head and studied me while running his tongue along his bottom lip. I knew the look.

"Something amiss, me deary?"

Why was he asking me? But they'd stopped for some reason, and I figured I should probably try and take advantage of it. I raised my chin and tried not to look at the dried saliva caking the wiry strands of his ginger beard.

"I need to pee."

His eyes dropped to my breasts as his lips stretched into a shallow grin.

"Why? We ain't gave you no water in a day."

"Please," I said, my voice much firmer than I felt.

He gave a grunt as one of the other Slavers trailed up next to him, younger than this guy, yet his tired snarl couldn't be hidden beneath the wide-brimmed hat pulled down low.

"Is there a problem?"

The ginger beard tore his eyes from my breasts.

"We should stop here to let them piss."

The younger man sneered. His gaze was the pointed fang of a snake bite, his smile the venom.

"They can wait. We'll make it before sundown if we keep pace."

"We'll make it before sundown either way," ginger beard said, his tone blunt as he ignored the glare of his companion and motioned for the others to prepare to unlock the cage.

The heels of his knee-high boots thumped against the dirt as he dismounted, his voice louder above the murmuring of prisoners who now felt entitled to urinate thanks to me. "You all have five minutes to do your business or you're shit out of luck—and I mean that literally!"

A few of our captors laughed while they yanked on the tethered shackles and pulled us through the unlocked door. The prisoners milled about after having the chains temporarily unlocked while the afternoon sun baked us, and the guards hurled insults along with the cracks of their whips. When you're a prisoner, modesty is a lost luxury, but I managed to slip behind a cluster of brown grass and do my business. It was when I stood that I caught sight of the prisoner with the wild eyes dawdling toward the front of the wagon.

I squinted and watched him for a minute.

With each step, his fingers twisted furiously while his hollowed eyes darted back and forth between the guards and the stretch of desert before him.

He couldn't be thinking of doing a runner?

A hawk circled above and a hot blast of air raced across the flat, empty desert. Nothing but low sage brush and rocks from the road to the horizon in every direction. Only the sweet aroma of pinion helped to mask the stench coming from us and that damn cage on the cart.

And boom. Just like that, he was off.

I was surprised at how much ground he covered with short, choppy strides before the guards noticed. He ran ahead, in the *same* direction we'd been traveling, which again made me wonder just how mushy his brain had become on our long journey. I held my breath. Based on what I'd seen and how I'd been treated, this was not going to end well for that kid. Desperation dulled the senses.

"Hey!"

My heart pounded as the guards yelled and snapped into action, releasing the hounds while some of the men mounted their horses and galloped off in pursuit. It only took a few seconds for them to catch up to him. A guard had begun rounding us up and moving us back toward the cart, which was where I soon stood with the other prisoners.

We watched in silence as the kid tried to kick at the dogs who snapped at him with foamy, bared teeth. One of the men on horseback cracked his whip, catching him on the temple.

The deranged boy screamed before falling to his hands and

knees. The guards circled him, each taking a club or hammer off their belts. One of them whistled and the dogs scurried back to allow the armed men to rain blows down upon the kid, pummeling his head and back, and then kicking at his ribs once he collapsed into the dirt.

A hand came up, fingers gnarled and covered in blood. Would that gesture be his final word? Just a simple sign of defiance? Submission? Reflex? The guards beat him unconscious before allowing the dogs back in the circle.

I closed my eyes to the sound of tearing flesh, grunting guards, and barking dogs. I silently begged for him to die, to escape the unbearable pain he'd suffer from those injuries for the rest of his life.

After the dogs had taken enough of his flesh to feed but not enough to kill him, the guards shackled his thin wrists and dragged his body over the hot sand to the wagon, throwing his bloody body into the cage.

The guards then turned on us, locking our shackles back to the chain and screaming at us to get back in, and that if we even thought about running, they'd let the dogs finish us off.

Not long after that stop, the cart slowed as we approached an ancient city that seemed to float above the shimmering sands of the Nevada territory. We rode beneath a faded, rusted sign.

"Nevada State Prison."

The painted arch sat atop massive iron gates with three guards on each side. After several seconds of shouting and insults exchanged between our guards and those at the gate, it opened with a low grind that made me shiver in the dry heat. They drove our cart through then, and I'll never forget the sound of the iron bars slamming back together, the chains being wrapped around the bars and the padlock clicking into place.

CONTINUE READING BATTLE CROW

Amazon

ABOUT KIM PETERSEN

Kim Petersen is a USA Today Bestselling and Award-winning author and editor of Medium publications Living Out Loud and SYNERGY. She is a top writer on Medium and co-author of *Creative Writing Energy: Tools to Access Your Higher-Creative Mind,* a book about alternative practices to help creatives rediscover and nurture their imaginative natural resources.

Her debut novel, *Millie's Angel,* received a gold award in the 2017 Dan Poynter's Global eBook Awards.

WEBSITE – AMAZON – TWITTER – FACEBOOK –
SUBSCRIBE

www.ingramcontent.com/pod-product-compliance
Lightning Source LLC
Chambersburg PA
CBHW021139130626
46554CB00005B/1578